Wh
at

"You can tell R.J. knows what it's like to live in the newspaper world, but with *Dead Shot*, he's proven that he also can write one heck of a murder mystery."

- Josh Katzowitz,
NFL writer for CBS.Sports.com
& author of Sid Gillman: Father of the Passing Game

DEAD LINE

"This book kept me on the edge of my seat the whole time. I didn't really want to put it down. R.J. Patterson has hooked me. I'll be back for more."

- Bob Behler
3-time Idaho broadcaster of the year
and play-by-play voice for Boise State football

BETTER OFF DEAD

A Novel

R.J. PATTERSON

Better Off Dead
© Copyright 2014 R.J. Patterson

First Print Edition 2013
Second Print Edtion 2014
Third Print Edition 2017

Cover Design by Dan Pitts

Previously published as Triple Cross

Published in the United States of America
Hangman Books
Boise Idaho 83713

For Gerald Guy, a real newspaper man

"Better a good journalist than a poor assassin."

- Jean-Paul Sartre

CHAPTER 1

AARON BANKS KNELT DOWN and looked into little Ethan's eyes. The joy plastered over Ethan's face reminded Aaron that his day off was his favorite day of the week. Not Sundays with thousands of fans worshipping him with each touchdown. Not the light practice days or the weekly Thursday afternoon hot tub soak with his teammates on the offensive line. Not even the days he went clubbing where gorgeous women threw themselves at him. Nope. The day that had nothing to do with football; yet it had everything to do with it. It was his day off, the day he visited the children's cancer ward of St. Mark's Hospital.

"You coming back to see me next week?" Ethan McCollister asked.

Aaron placed his palm on the top of the nine-year-old boy's bald head. He rubbed the top of Ethan's scalp and made a squeaky noise with his mouth. It always led to Ethan giggling.

"Sure thing, little buddy," Aaron said. "I wouldn't miss it for anything."

Aaron stood his strapping 6-foot-3, 240-pound frame upright and announced his intention to exit the room as he waved good-bye. Suddenly, a group of about ten kids rushed Aaron, waving and telling him they couldn't wait to see him next week. Aaron gently loosened the grip of Grace Blackwell, who viewed his leg as a mode of transportation more for her than him.

Every week he considered how much easier it would be to slip out without a word, but he even enjoyed it when the kids swarmed him as he left. Aaron managed to create enough space between him and the kids with his best stiff arm as he walked backward to the door. He winked at Cindy Lassiter, his favorite pediatric nurse, and flashed her his multi-million dollar endorsement smile. He finally made it out of the room and secured the door behind him.

Aaron always noted how his problems disappeared during the two hours each week when he visited the hospital. But the moment he walked through the hospital's automatic doors and back into the warm L.A. sun, those problems hit him harder than a lead pipe to the head. He often lamented the loss of simpler times, those periods where football, friends, and family filled his life. Friends who he enjoyed. Family who cherished him simply because they were family. Football that was fun. But those days were a distant memory. Now life consisted of determining if his so-called friends cared about him or his money, and family who only came around when they wanted a handout. Football was about playing just well enough to stay on a roster and avoid getting overtaken by the latest new rookie star. His dream of playing pro football devolved into an inescapable nightmare.

Aaron dug into his pocket and fished out the twelfth picture Ethan had drawn of him scoring a touchdown. After Ethan heard Aaron donated $10,000 to the hospital for every touchdown he scored, the young cancer patient struck a deal with his favorite player: A hand-drawn picture of every touchdown he scored. Aaron smiled at the way Ethan had depicted him leaping into the end zone. Everything looked accurate, except the addition of a cape. Ethan always added a special touch. The art would hang in Aaron's *defacto* hallway art gallery, a daily reminder of what really made his life count.

With the rest of Aaron's life seeming more burdensome, he knew he could simply quit, walk away from the millions and disappear from public life. But then he wouldn't have the game he loved—or those two inspirational hours every week. In the previous season, Aaron missed four games with complications from an ankle injury. Instead of being annoyed at having to sit out, he used that extra time to visit St. Mark's every day for a month. It was heaven. But he knew after he left football, the next group of kids in the cancer ward would have no idea who he was and wonder why he came to visit them. So he would tolerate the other 166 hours of his week for these two. No cost was too high for two hours of such delight, for two hours of meaningful living.

Aaron sank into the leather driver's seat of his black McLaren F1. He turned the ignition as the engine roared to life. The F1 was his one guilty pleasure in an otherwise modest lifestyle. He stomached the city's glorified celebrity culture, but he didn't embrace it like some of his other teammates. Starved for a pro football team for far too long, L.A. begged, bribed and cajoled the NFL to expand and add the L.A. Stars to the league. The expansion draft resulted in a team comprised of rookies and former superstars. L.A. sports fans cared about winning, but more people just cared about having a new subset of celebrities to adore. Aaron liked to think of himself as one of the younger stars on the team, but at age 30, who was he kidding? He was a long-toothed veteran. He knew his prime years were likely behind him. Another year or two worth of incredible off days and then it would end. It was an end that should have arrived already. He wanted to fight it, but not the way they made him do it. It was on their terms. He had no choice.

He glanced at the *Sports Illustrated* Sportsman of the Year edition behind him in one of the car's two passenger seats. He was on the cover two years ago. He kept the magazine with him to remind him of who he was, who he wanted to be—not who he had become. Winning the league's rushing crown made him a hot commodity in charity circles a few years ago. Everyone wanted him to lend his name to their cause. So he did. It made him feel good to do something more than just regularly visit a hospital. His good looks and winning smile made his face synonymous with a cause, any cause. But being a do-gooder wore him out. He wanted to help, but it cluttered his life and made his weekly visits to St. Mark's feel like just another appointment in his busy schedule. So like a desperate addict trying to break free, he quit cold turkey. No more lending his name to charities or his picture. He just wanted to work with kids and have fun, not become an icon for raising money for starving children in Africa. He caught himself staring at L.A.'s smoggy skyline, wondering to himself, "If those kids ever found out who I really am …"

His phone rang, snapping him back to the present. It was his agent, Bobby Franklin.

"What's up, big man?" Aaron answered.

"Just ready to destroy some ribs at Jackson's and talk some business," Bobby said.

Aaron recognized the tactic right away—use his favorite barbecue restaurant to soften the blow of some difficult news. "Business? What kind of business?"

"Oh, you know. The kind that you don't want to talk about."

Aaron grew agitated at Bobby's shroud of secrecy. "Out with it, Bobby. What is it?"

"Oh, it's nothing we can't fix."

"Just say it, Bobby. You know I hate it when you do this."

"OK, I got a call from your general manager and he gave me a heads up that you aren't going to fit in the Stars' plans next year. They're going to release you at the end of the season."

"What? Why? I've got two years left on my contract. They can't do that."

"Yes, they can, Aaron. And they're going to. Before you get mad, you should appreciate the courtesy they gave us with this heads up. It will help us get you positioned for the best situation with another team next season."

"I don't want to play anywhere but here next season!"

"Look, I know you're upset about this. But just calm down and let's talk about it, OK?"

Aaron's phone buzzed with another call.

"Fine. I've got another call coming in that I need to take. I'll meet you at Jackson's in half an hour."

Aaron switched over to the other line.

"Hey. Are we meeting at the usual spot?"

"Yeah," came the voice on the other end. "See you there in ten minutes."

Aaron hung up and peeled out of the St. Mark's parking lot. His greatest pain followed his greatest joy each week—picking up his performance enhancing drugs: PEDs. He laughed at the grandiose promise of the name. *Performance enhancing. Ha! You still have to do all the work. What a joke!*

Aaron loathed putting anything in his body that wasn't natural with the exception of lip-smacking smoked ribs slathered in barbecue sauce. That made his decision to go along with the Stars' request to use PEDs that much more difficult. It wasn't really a request, more like an ultimatum, the kind some grimy guy delivers who isn't on the team's official payroll. He even set up a clandestine rendezvous point in a warehouse parking lot to get his monthly supply.

That's where Aaron was headed as he veered north onto the 5 and shifted the car into a higher gear and mashed the gas. With each upward shift, Aaron jammed the stick with more force. *How could they do this to me after all I've done for them? I don't fit in their plans? I'll show them!*

When Aaron finally arrived in the warehouse parking lot, he skidded to a stop and climbed out of his car. He stormed toward his supplier, kicking up dust and small rocks in his wake. He grabbed the handle on the driver's door and yanked it open.

"Get out now!" Aaron screamed.

The supplier put his hands up in surrender. "Relax, Aaron. No need to be so aggressive."

"Oh, really. Do you know what's going on?"

"So, you're upset that the team is moving on without you. I get that. But it's no reason to go crazy." The man began to slowly get out of his car.

Aaron grabbed a fistful of the man's shirt and flung him against his car.

"Crazy?! Crazy?! I'm not crazy—I'm angry! I've been used by this organization. I'm done with this." He released the man's shirt. "It's over for me, but it's just starting for them."

Aaron turned and stormed toward his car. He grabbed the handgun he kept in his glove compartment. In his other hand, he clutched the pills. He got out of his car and stood near the driver's side.

Bam!

The running back slumped to the ground, dead before he hit it. PED pills scattered around his body on the ground along with the empty bottle.

CHAPTER 2

CAL STARED BLANKLY at his computer terminal. It stared back at him, also blank. There was writer's block—and then there was story block. The former was reserved for novelists or other writers who were in love with each word they banged out on a keyboard. The latter was reserved for journalists. No matter how well you wrote, it mattered little if there were no good stories to tell.

"Hey, Cal. Have I got a story for you," bellowed a voice across the newsroom.

Cal rolled his eyes and sighed. He spun around to see Stan Hardman walking toward him with a sheet of paper in one hand and a goofy grin on his face. Cal considered that being drawn and quartered might be less painful than facing Hardman's mockery to start his Monday morning.

"What is it, Hardman?" Cal mumbled.

"I just got a fax from the Bay Area Chess Club that Harold Weinholtz is retiring. He had been in that position 35 years. Now, I'm not nearly as good of an investigative reporter as you are, but I bet there's more to the story. I'm sure readers will want to know if he retired on his own or was forced out? And if he was forced out, why? This could be another award winner for you."

Cal glared at Hardman. "I'm not in the mood."

"I'm just trying to help, Cal. I know it's been a while since you had a big story that landed you on the front page. Heck, it's been a while since you landed a story in the paper anywhere. So, don't be too quick to dismiss this."

Cal caught the smile creeping up at the corners of Hardman's mouth. It was a mouth he wanted to punch. He snatched the fax from Hardman and jammed it into his trashcan.

"Was that too quick?" Cal snarled.

"Suit yourself," Hardman said before turning around and walking back toward his cubicle.

As much as Cal loathed Hardman and his incessant mocking, the San Francisco *Chronicle's* top sports columnist was right: it had been far too long since Cal wrote anything noteworthy.

After winning several national writing awards in a period of three years, Cal felt lost. Deep down, he knew he had stumbled onto his award-winning pieces, but who wouldn't parlay such luck into a big payday at a prestigious newspaper? He reported on athletes who did it every day. One good season right before you became a free agent and suddenly every general manager forgot how horrible you were and overpaid you to get you on his roster. Then when you go back to being mediocre, everyone hates you—the fans, the reporters, the sports talk radio guys. You were lucky to have your mom still like you. That's all that Cal did. Two great stories and editors began fighting for him. *The Chronicle* won. Cal should have expected a backlash like this. He certainly never minded dishing out such criticism to athletes who did the same thing. But it didn't feel fair now that he was the one on the receiving end of the vitriol. It felt far more personal than he imagined, like he was a fraud.

Once *The Chronicle* hired Cal, he was tasked with writing enterprise and investigative pieces. They were lengthy articles, written in long form style. They told compelling stories about a person or a program. Maybe a cautionary tale of a fallen star athlete. Or a portrait of a long-time athletic director at an inner city school. Or a historical piece on the University of San Francisco's back-to-back national championships in basketball during the 1950s. They showcased Cal's writing prowess, but not the real reason he was hired. Anyone on *The Chronicle*'s talented sports staff could have written those articles as well as Cal. Those assignments were supposed to fill the time until he broke a story that rocked the sports world. Instead, that was all he was writing. He wasn't breaking anything but *The Chronicle's* cash-strapped budget. Rumors were already swirling about another round of newsroom layoffs coming within the next six months. Cal knew if he didn't produce something of value, he would be gone.

Cal checked his watch then grabbed his computer bag. He had a meeting in fifteen minutes with a guy who said he had something big. The man told Cal it would blow the lid on one of the best-kept secrets in sports. Most of the time these so-called tips turned out to be a joke, more suited for those who wore fitted tin-foil hats. But Cal oozed desperation like a 45-year-old single woman at a college town bar. He couldn't let any prospect get away, no matter how ridiculous it sounded.

He breezed past Hardman's desk, but not so fast that the columnist didn't notice.

"In a hurry, Cal?" Hardman asked. "Got another tip from a little old lady about how the 49ers threw that game to the Raiders?"

"Shove it, Hardman." Cal didn't look back. No use giving Hardman's giant ego the pleasure of knowing the barbs were getting to him.

Cal opted for the stairwell over the elevators. He galloped down the stairs and walked through the lobby into the busy San Francisco business district. He was still a block away from the coffee shop on Fifth and Market when his phone buzzed.

He looked at the caller ID and smiled.

"Kelly," he answered. "How are you?"

"Fantastic, Cal. And yourself?"

"Oh, I've had better days."

"Well, I hope we can have a few good ones over Thanksgiving this weekend. You're still planning on coming, right?"

Writing another award-winning story wasn't the only objective derailed in Cal's life at the moment. He longed to be in the same city with Kelly again, just a few months of dating like normal people to figure out if maybe she was the one. They had been through a lot together but they never could seem to land in the same place. He thought San Francisco would be the place when they were both offered jobs there—Cal at *The Chronicle*, Kelly as the assistant photo editor at the Associated Press bureau. Cal accepted the job and so did Kelly. But two days before Kelly was scheduled to move, a photo editor much senior than her requested a transfer to San Francisco to be with her ailing mother. Kelly wound up in Los Angeles instead. Cal settled for short plane trips and long weekends to see her.

"Oh, I'll be there all right. It's not like there's any big story for me to cover here. Unless, of course, you consider the resignation of Harold Weinholtz from his position as the president of the Bay Area Chess Club as the beginnings of some great investigative piece?"

"Sounds like you've got your hands full," Kelly chided. "I'll pick you up from LAX on Wednesday night."

Cal exchanged goodbyes with Kelly and ended the call before letting his mind drift. He wanted to be with her, wherever that was. And as much as he liked San Francisco, Cal certainly wasn't going to leave his heart here this weekend. It longed to be with a certain leggy brunette on some deserted beach in the South Pacific. Or this weekend—with her in L.A.

A taxi horn blared, snapping Cal back to the present. He glanced up at the television hanging in the cafe to see a news report about another shocking suicide of a pro football player, this time the L.A. Stars' Aaron Banks. These suicides were happening with such regularity that it barely moved anyone's shock meter anymore. Another pro football player, another suicide. But this was an active player, who still possessed star power. Cal wondered what could have been that bad about Banks' life that he had to end it. He checked his watch. It was noon and he began searching for the man he was meeting. Cal felt a sudden poke in his back.

"Are you Cal?"

"Yes," Cal said as he began to turn around to greet the man. Then he stopped. The poke felt a little stiffer, digging further into Cal's back.

"Don't turn around. It's best that you can't identify me— for both our sake."

Cal didn't like this introduction. He almost walked away without uttering another word but decided it might be worth listening to the man's kooky conspiracy. If anything, it would make for a good story at the next dinner party he attended. Cal was just too curious.

"OK, fine," Cal said resisting the urge to look at the man. "What is this big conspiracy you mentioned?"

"Almost every player on the L.A. Stars is using PEDs and the lab I work for is covering it up. You'll know I'm telling the truth when word leaks out that Aaron Banks was using, too."

"Why are you telling me this?"

There was a long pause. "It's complicated, but I'm tired of living a lie."

"But why me?" Cal demanded.

He played to Cal's ego. "I heard you were the best."

Cal liked this conspiracy's potential but he needed something more than an accusation from a secretive whistleblower.

"You got any proof?"

Cal felt the poke in his back get a little stiffer.

"Take this thumb drive. It contains PDFs of all the failed tests, but don't leak these out until you have more evidence. It'll come back to me and they'll kill me."

Cal reached behind him to take the thumb drive from the informant's hand.

"Who will kill you?" Cal asked.

The man said nothing. Cal waited a few more seconds before he turned around. There was nobody behind him. More patrons twisted and cavorted their bodies through the narrow openings in the shop jammed with lunchtime customers. Cal had no way of identifying the man now, but it didn't matter if the evidence in his hand was legit.

Cal glanced back up at the television and strained to listen to the news report on the television. When he couldn't discern what the reporter was saying through the buzz of conversation, he squinted to read the white words crawling through the red stripe at the bottom of the screen:

Sources: NFL was set to suspend deceased L.A. Stars' running back Aaron Banks for failing a drug test.

Cal caught himself smiling and then stopped. He hated the fact that his greatest fortune in life came at the hands of someone else's misfortune. But he couldn't help it. It was his job. Then Cal started smiling again.

CHAPTER 3

CHARLES ROBINSON STOOD UP and stretched before slumping back down into his executive leather chair. At 65 years old, he still didn't appear to be a day over 50. At six-foot-one, Robinson flaunted his height, but not as much as his chiseled frame. He wore tight shirts that put his bulging muscles on display. With thick brown hair slicked back and a clean shaven face, Robinson thought he and his piercing blue eyes might find a home in Hollywood if this business venture failed.

Robinson's office contained all the decadent décor everyone expected the owner of an NFL team to have. Oak paneled walls. Plush leather couches and chairs. Framed jerseys and pictures of past and current NFL stars. A small Stars' replica helmet on the corner of his desk. Then there was Robinson's personalized touch of a lion's head mounted on one of the walls. He shot the lion on a big game hunt in Zimbabwe several years ago and wasn't going to let anyone forget about it or leave out the fact that he shot it from 250 yards away.

He then spun around in his chair.

In stark contrast to his office was the drab industrial park serving as a backdrop for the Stars' outdated stadium. What was once a crown jewel among professional stadiums was now a clunker of a home field. The luxury boxes held no aesthetic value. The emissions that wafted over the field frequently served as a constant reminder that for all of Hollywood's glitz and glamour, the only thing about this franchise that said "L.A." was the team's name. It stopped cold right there.

But Robinson knew how to fix all of this. His ability to take a dog of a company and turn it into a champion was legendary. With the L.A. Stars, the answer was quite simple: win.

Win and the money pours in. Win and people will do whatever you want them to. Win and you dictate the terms. But lose? Then you have nothing. For Robinson, *nothing* wasn't an option.

When Robinson bought the right to own and start the team five years ago, he figured just having a team in America's largest city that had gone so long without one would be enough for a while. And it was. But after a while, expectations change. People begin expecting you to win. That's what happened to all the other teams in L.A. before the Stars. They started losing and fans lost interest. Robinson understood this important piece of the city's history along with this reality: this is SoCal and there are far better ways to spend your Sunday afternoon and your money than by watching a crumby team play in a rundown stadium on a crime-ridden part of town.

Near the end of their fourth season in existence, the Stars were last in their division again. The local sports columnists questioned every move the coaches made. Local sports talk radio skewered the team's play. The social media scene kept tabs on the players and tweeted photos of them out partying after losses. He fully expected the fans who attended to the final game of that season to show up with more torches and pitchforks than tickets.

But this was L.A., where fortunes can rise and fall faster than a starlet enters and exits rehab. One week your movie is number one, the next week you are recorded making drunken slurs. It was a place where anyone can make a comeback, no matter how long you've been cast aside.

Robinson put into motion a plan for a comeback of his own, the kind that would make people forget about the Stars' losing ways. He wanted his team to be the talk of the town. Lakers? Clippers? Dodgers? Angels? Kings? Ducks? None of them would garner the media attention one juggernaut NFL team would. That was the goal. All smart billionaires use their money to make more money. But like the brightest of billionaires, Robinson wanted to use the people's money to make himself more money. He understood the quickest way to increase your wealth is to figure out a way to increase your reward without increasing your risk.

For a man who made a vast fortune by creating a powerful media conglomerate, Robinson was both smart and brilliant. He knew that if the Stars were winning, interest in the team would soar and so would the advertising rates associated with anything that had to do with the team. C.R. Enterprises owned more than a dozen newspapers in California, eight of them in Southern California in and around Los Angeles. He also owned several radio stations, including the flagship station of the Stars and the city's best sports talk station. Then there were his television stations. Even his specialty websites flourished. If you learned about anything that happened in Southern California, it was likely from some media arm of C.R. Enterprises.

Robinson used his media influence to control the Stars' narrative as best as he could. When the team struggled, the media relations personnel leaked information about injuries to star players. When there was dissention in the clubhouse, Robinson made sure there was some other story that overshadowed the locker room backbiting—even if the story was fabricated. He even planted "fans" to catch his star players helping the community. The media and fans had no idea how they were being manipulated. But Robinson knew his control could only last so long. He needed the Stars to morph into winners so he could get his new stadium. And morphing they were, leading the division by two games with five games left in the season. The playoffs were almost a lock.

The intercom on Robinson's desk phone beeped and his assistant notified him of the caller holding for him. It was Los Angeles city councilman Mel Moore.

"Good morning, Mel. Are you going to join me in my box on Sunday?" Robinson asked.

Mel sighed before speaking. "Look, Charles. I don't think that's a good idea. I don't want to give off the wrong impression."

"What? That you're a fan of L.A.'s only pro football team?"

"No, no. I just don't want anyone to think you bought my vote."

Robinson smiled. "So, this means you're voting to approve the new stadium at next week's vote?"

"Of course, Charles. I just don't want to see this deal sabotaged by the media if they start sniffing around."

"Mel, are you forgetting that I *am* the media in this town? I understand your concern, but let's not worry about that anymore. Nobody is going to write in any of my papers that your vote was bought. And we both know my papers are the only ones anybody in this town reads anyway."

"No, I haven't forgotten that. Nor have I forgotten all those discounted ads you gave us during the election last year. That's why I'm voting to approve. But let's be wise about this, OK? I don't care that you control the media, all it takes is one rogue reporter to blow the whole thing up in this day and age."

"OK, no box seats for you, but I will leave a pair of tickets for you at will call. See you next week at the hearing."

Robinson hung up the phone. He didn't want to wait to hear Moore's forthcoming protest. He had the confirmation he wanted. In less than a week, the Stars' new stadium was about to be approved. Hollywood demanded nothing but extravagance. And both the princes and paupers of this town would pay for it.

This news called for a private celebration—immediately.

Robinson walked across his office to his bar and pulled out his finest scotch—a bottle of Glenfarclas 1955, reserved for the rarest of occasions. It was still unopened. In just under five years, Robinson achieved his goal of securing a new stadium for the Stars. That's how he always did things. He set a goal and he achieved it. Then he would set another goal and achieve it, too. Robinson dwelt in the white collar world, but he possessed blue collar work habits. Do what it takes to get the job done every single day. Don't let anyone stand in your way. Robinson had left tread marks all over anyone who dared to challenge him. Now it was time to take a moment and enjoy his Scotch before moving to his next most important objective, one that would make him more money than he ever imagined possible.

CHAPTER 4

CAL WHISTLED AS HE walked through the sports department, clutching the thumb drive he collected from his mysterious informant. He glanced at Hardman, who was spinning around in his chair to fire off a snarky comment.

"Save it, Hardman," Cal snapped. "You'll regret it after I wrap up this award-winning story."

Hardman laughed. He couldn't resist a good jab. "I knew there was more to that Bay Area Chess Club story. Kudos for landing something printable."

Cal turned and glared at him, offering no response. His mind was already on the story that had just been handed to him. All he had to do was put the pieces of the puzzle together.

He sat down at his desk and inserted the thumb drive into his computer. He clicked on the drive's folder and began opening a slew of PDFs. File after file consisted of failed drug tests. But there was one problem: all the names had been redacted. It was always the biggest problem for getting any requests filled through Freedom of Information Acts. They were like an endless game of fill-in-the-blank Mad Libs. The first time Cal received FOIA documents, he threw a tirade on the spot, demanding to get a copy without the names. Privacy concerns and poorly written requests allowed government agencies to hide the identities of most people. After spending a month trying to track down all empty blanks, Cal decided to scan the document and see if he could use Photoshop to decipher the names. It worked. He began employing his tactic to scoop other journalists on several breaking news stories. However, when a government worker figured out what Cal was doing, all government agencies nationwide switched to markers that left no discernable words—not even using genius computer programs.

Cal immediately made two copies of the files, one to his computer's hard drive and another to a thumb drive. He then called one of the staff photographers, Mike Gregory.

"You busy?" Cal asked.

"Not at the moment. What do you need?" Gregory replied.

"I need a favor on a story I'm working on. I need your Photoshop wizardry on this one."

"OK, fill me in and I'll see what I can do."

Cal hustled down one flight of stairs to the photo department. Mike's desk was the first one in the vast cubicle farm.

Cal held out the thumb drive and handed it to Gregory. "I need you to help me decipher the redacted names on this file."

"Oh, come on, Cal. I'm a photographer, not a miracle worker."

Cal was ready for the pushback. "This isn't a Freedom of Information Act requested document. This was put together by a guy who I'm not sure knew what he was doing. He didn't use the magic pen, OK?"

Gregory snatched the thumb drive from Cal and shot him a skeptical glance. He began opening the files.

"What is this, Cal?"

"I had an informant give this to me today. He said it was a bunch of failed drug tests from NFL players."

"Oh, wonderful. When are you guys just going to give up on the steroid witch hunt and just enjoy the juiced game like the rest of us?"

Cal smiled. "Maybe when it's legal to use the stuff? I don't make the rules. But cheating always makes for a good scandalous story."

Gregory wasn't amused. He said nothing but began a whirl-wind of mouse movements and clicks. It took Gregory less than a minute to get the first name to come into focus: Isaiah Smith.

"Isaiah Smith? Quarterback of the L.A. Stars?" Gregory asked.

"That would be the one. Try another one."

A few clicks and keystrokes later and Aaron Banks' name appeared on the screen.

"Isn't this the kid that killed himself this week?" Gregory asked.

"Yep. That's him. What's the date on his?"

"November 10th."

"Wow. That was just two weeks ago."

Gregory went back to the first file. "Isaiah's is dated November 10th as well."

"Yeah, and only Banks is being reported as having flunked a drug test. Do you think you can print out Banks' form for me and clear the rest of these up when you get a chance and email them to me?"

"You got it, Cal."

"Thanks. Later."

Cal waited a few seconds to grab Banks' failed drug test form and head back upstairs to the sports department. He wasted no time knocking on his editor's door.

"Miles Kennedy" was the name painted on the glass door. Kennedy wasn't an imposing editor, but he could be a bulldog when the situation required it. At five-foot-six, Kennedy wasn't exactly the poster child for modern health. He scarfed down San Francisco's greasiest cuisine nightly, washing it all down with at least several beers a night. If things got stressful around the office, Kennedy went for the bottle of bourbon hidden beneath his file folder.

Cal was grateful for the time Kennedy had given him to adjust to the new work environment, but in the past few weeks,

Cal started to feel the heat. He understood favoritism only lasted so long—at some point, he needed to write a blockbuster story. Budget cuts were coming, dictating more layoffs. And Cal needed to come up big with a story—and soon.

Kennedy motioned for Cal to enter his cramped office.

"What you got, Cal?" Kennedy asked. "Anything I can lead with tomorrow?"

"Maybe not tomorrow, but certainly something that could rock the sports world."

"Oh? Start talking. What's the story?"

"You know that Aaron Banks guy that just committed suicide?"

"Yeah. He's from the Bay area."

"Well, I just had a source give me this failed drug test. But he wasn't the only one."

Cal launched into an explanation of the events that had transpired over the past two hours.

Kennedy spoke cautiously. "So, you've got redacted files from an unknown, unidentifiable source and a hunch?"

Cal nodded sheepishly. When Kennedy broke down the pitch, Cal's great story idea sounded more like something from an obscure blog site written by a guy wearing NFL pajamas living in his mom's basement.

"So, you got only a tad more than nothing?" Kennedy asked rhetorically.

"I know it sounds crazy, but let me poke around on this, OK? Let me see if something comes up?"

Kennedy grimaced and rubbed his face with both hands.

"OK. You've got until Monday. If you don't have anything more substantial by then, you're off this story."

Cal thanked him and turned toward the door.

Kennedy wasn't finished.

"Cal, I have to be honest with you. I don't want to let you go, but I'll have to unless you give me a good reason I can take to the higher ups. More layoffs are coming and unfortunately, you're on the short list for our department. If I had my druthers, I'd keep you around."

"I understand," Cal said.

"I'm not trying to put any undue pressure on you, but I figured you would appreciate me being real with you about the situation."

Cal nodded knowingly and exited Kennedy's office. He didn't dwell on the last part of his conversation with Kennedy. He already knew that. Cal was already thinking about this story, something he needed to save his job.

He returned to his desk and dialed the number for Pacific Laboratories.

"PacLabs. My name is Jenny. How may I assist you?"

"Hi, Jenny. My name is Cal Murphy from *The Chronicle*. Do you guys give tours?"

"No. Sorry, but we don't."

"Is there anyone I can speak to? I have a few questions about a story I'm working on."

"Everyone in our media relations department is out right now, but if you leave me your contact info, I will pass it along."

Cal gave her his info but he never expected a call back. He would have to pay PacLabs a visit if he wanted some answers.

CHAPTER 5

TED SIMPSON PUT ON his lab coat and returned to processing drug tests. His hands began shaking so uncontrollably that he nearly spilled a sample. He let out a big sigh and tried to regain his composure.

"You OK, Ted?" one of his fellow lab assistants asked.

"Yeah. Just dealing with a lot right now. But I'm good."

Like the rest of his life, Ted's answer was only half true. He was dealing with plenty. His brother, Tommy, was suffering from a rare pulmonary disease and was constantly flirting with death. He had no other family since both his parents died when he was 14.

Ted appeared to be on the road for tremendous success career wise after graduating from college. He worked at a startup with a few of his college friends that started to take off. Then Ted's brother fell ill. No matter how much money Ted made, it wasn't enough to sustain his brother's rising medical costs. That's when the human resources director for PacLabs contacted Ted about a job. At first, Ted hesitated to leave his startup, but PacLabs quickly convinced him to leave and sealed the deal by agreeing to cover Tommy's medical expenses. The company also agreed to help Tommy by also paying for an experimental treatment. Ted saw no reason to question PacLabs' generosity. He thought it was an incredible gesture from a company that valued its employees and their loyalty. But he quickly learned that their loyalty came at a costly price.

Ted thought about his brother. It was a bond strong enough to cause Ted to forfeit almost every virtue he valued. Almost from day one, Ted realized this job consisted of much more than he imagined. He wasn't sure if he could do what they asked him at first, but he concluded Tommy's life was worth it. So he gritted his teeth and did it—but he wasn't proud of it.

Over time as Ted's conscience began to gnaw at him, he began gathering evidence. He shuddered to think what would happen to him if they caught him. He wondered about Tommy and if the doctors might remove him from the experimental treatment once he went public with this information. He wondered if he could find another job in this economy. Exposing PacLabs didn't make rational sense. Just go along with it. Don't butcher your milk cow. That was conventional wisdom. And Ted was tired of exercising conventional wisdom. That's why he went to Cal Murphy—and that's why his answer to his colleague was only half true. He was trying to be good *and* do good, but he felt anything but good at the moment.

"Ted, can you go check the front desk for those samples we were supposed to get today? Jenny's been slacking lately," came the request from the lab supervisor.

"Yeah. No problem," Ted answered as he began walking toward the door.

Ted always liked talking with Jenny, even if she was spacey. In Ted's mind, blonde hair, blue eyes and a tight body made up for plenty of shortcomings—even if none of it was natural. He tried to flirt with her, but she never reciprocated. She was all business with the lab techs.

"Hey, Jenny. Have you got any specimens for me?"

"Uh, no. I would call you if I did." She paused. "And why do you have to call them specimens? That's just gross."

"That's what we call them in the lab, Jenny. That's what they are."

"Well, that's just disgusting."

Before Ted's failed attempt at flirting went any further into the abyss, he looked up and froze.

Cal Murphy was standing in the lobby.

* * *

When Cal walked into the PacLabs lobby, he surveyed the environment. White. Modern. Sterile. Nothing about the place suggested he sit and stay a while. He started to walk toward the receptionist's desk when a guy in a white lab coat looked at him and quickly put his head down and dashed down the hallway. Cal immediately knew the guy was his snitch. Now all he needed was his name and he needed to get it in the most discreet way possible.

Cal walked up to the edge of his receptionist's desk and flashed a warm smile.

"Boyfriend?" Cal asked, gesturing with his eyes toward the man bumbling down the hall.

"Him?" she asked in a tone suggesting Cal wasn't serious.

Cal nodded.

"No, that's just awkward Ted," she said. "To be honest, most of the guys here are awkward—and single. But I haven't found one that's my taste yet."

"So the odds are good but the goods are odd?" Cal asked.

Jenny furrowed her brow, unaware his response was a joke, subtle or otherwise.

"Never mind. I didn't come here to talk about your love life. I actually came here to see if I could speak with someone who could answer a few questions for me for a story I'm working on regarding NFL drug testing."

"OK, Mister —"

"Murphy. Cal Murphy from *The Chronicle*."

"Let me check."

Jenny began pressing buttons on her master switchboard telephone. Cal leaned on the desk and cut his eyes down toward her phone. He noticed about 40 names assigned to buttons, including the name of "Ted Simpson."

Cal wasn't paying attention to her conversation and was almost unaware it had ended until she said his name.

"Mr. Murphy, I'm sorry, but no one is here who can help you right now. I can have someone contact you later."

"OK, that's fine. I called earlier but I was in the neighborhood and thought I would stop by in person. I'll just await your call."

He casually turned and headed toward the door. He already had what he came for.

CHAPTER 6

MILES KENNEDY DRUMMED HIS FINGERS on his desk as he surveyed the story budget for the next day's sports section. Selecting the top story pained him on this day. Aaron Banks had grown up in the Bay Area. He was Mr. Football for *The Chronicle* his senior year of high school and his scholarship signing was aired live on ESPN. There was no doubt he was a popular player and his paper had followed his every career move for the past fifteen years. That's what made his decision even tougher. Did he really want to blare Banks' suicide across the front of the section? Kennedy's humanity chipped away at his newspaper soul when stories like these appeared in the news cycle.

His phone rang, breaking his moment of torturous solitude.

"Kennedy."

"Mr. Kennedy, my name is Aretha Banks and I wanted to talk to you about something."

Kennedy sat up in his chair and readied his pen to take notes.

"Mrs. Banks, let me first give you my condolences on the death of your son. Aaron was a great guy and I enjoyed every encounter I had with him."

"Thank you for telling me that, Mr. Kennedy. But I have something to ask of you. I know it may sound crazy or just like an insane mama grieving the loss of her son, but I'm serious when I say this. I want you to investigate Aaron's death because there's no way he killed himself."

Kennedy was taken aback by her comment. "I understand you're grieving and I don't want to be insensitive when I ask this, Mrs. Banks, but what makes you think someone killed him?"

"He would never do that. Ever. And he wouldn't do drugs either. I taught him better than that. He still had the rest of his life ahead of him and I'm not buying everything that's being sold by the media and the LAPD."

"Look, we're not investigators, per se. And there are limits to what information we can obtain, but I do have a reporter who is working on a story about Aaron and you could talk to him about it."

Kennedy gave her Cal's information and hung up. His first reaction was assuming Mrs. Banks was just like any other mother. But the more he thought about it, the more he started to believe maybe Cal was onto something and maybe there was a bigger story looming. However, it did nothing to solve how he would handle tomorrow's front page.

* * *

Stopped at a traffic light, Cal looked at his buzzing phone. He didn't recognize the number and sent it to voicemail. He debated cancelling his trip to see Kelly in L.A., but the more he thought about it, the more he was sure that he needed to go there to get the full story. There was only so much investigating he could do in San Francisco, especially with the weekend rapidly approaching. The light turned green.

Nothing mattered right now except for the name Ted Simpson. Who was this guy? What drove him to being a snitch? Cal needed a fuller picture of his subject before he began giving him the first degree. This was priority number one when he returned to the office.

Stopped at a traffic light, Cal tapped his hands on the steering wheel to one of his favorite Jay-Z songs. His love for hip hop was a newly acquired taste in music and he dove headlong into the genre. After watching a few Jay-Z videos, he learned that shaking your head too vigorously was a sign that you were not a true connoisseur of hip hop. Instead, you needed to nod your head ever so slightly to the beat of the music.

I got ninety-nine problems …

If Jay-Z had ninety-nine problems, Cal felt like he had at least 100, maybe more. Talking to Ted Simpson and getting him to go on record might solve the most important of those problems.

Bam!

Cal's car lurched forward.

Great. Make that a hundred and one problems!

Cal stopped and looked in the rearview mirror, noticing a not-so-pleasant looking driver sitting behind the wheel of a black Hummer H2. With visible tattoos and a Fu Manchu moustache, the man remained in his vehicle, snarling at Cal. The light turned green and the growing line of cars at the light behind him began laying on their horns and shouting.

Cal ignored them and got out of his car. He walked toward the vehicle behind him before the driver of the H2 saluted Cal with his middle finger and roared away. Cal continued to walk to the back of his car to inspect the damage. Nothing major. A slight dent and some scratched paint. More cars pulled around Cal's stationary vehicle. More drivers yelled nasty things at Cal.

Ah, California. Gotta love these people.

Flustered, Cal returned to his car. It was a hit-and-run accident, but it likely wouldn't meet his deductible, so he didn't bother calling the police or reporting it. Just another inconvenience to deal with next week after he came back from L.A.

Cal turned off Jay-Z and decided to listen to his voicemail. It was Mrs. Banks.

"Mr. Murphy, my name is Aretha Banks. Your kind boss

gave me your number and said you were working on a story about Aaron. I told him and I'll tell you—Aaron would not kill himself. Nor would he do drugs. I can't get a straight answer from anyone at the LAPD about his death. Please call me if you get a chance. I need to talk with you."

Cal figured if Kennedy passed his contact info along then he knew about this. Maybe his crazy hunch was turning into the legitimate story he needed—and the story Kennedy hired him to find two years ago.

Now Cal knew he needed to go to L.A. for sure. The smoke was sure to reveal a raging fire somewhere.

Cal approached another intersection and checked his rearview mirror. Then he checked again. Dominating the mirror was the black H2 that ran into him earlier, driven by the same jerk. The man gave Cal the cut-throat sign and flashed an evil grin. The H2 was two cars behind him, but Cal started to shutter. Is this guy just a world-class maniac or is he really following me?

Cal looked in his mirror again. This time, the man brandished a pistol and was pointing it right at Cal.

The light turned green and Cal stomped on the gas. He started to get that sick eerie feeling he always got when he began digging into a story that he knew nobody wanted unearthed.

* * *

Charles Robinson swiveled around in his chair to answer his cell phone.

"What is it?" he asked.

"We've got a problem," came the reply.

"What kind of problem?"

"A rat."

"Well, you know what to do."

Robinson slammed his phone down. He didn't need any problems. Not this week, anyway. He was too close to moving into phase 2 of his plan for anyone to stop him.

CHAPTER 7

CAL ARRIVED BACK AT the office and didn't even acknowledge Hardman's stale chess-related barb as he breezed through the cubicle farm to his desk. He sat down and began pounding in the name "Ted Simpson" along with "lab research" into a Google search.

Bingo!

Ted Simpson graduated from Berkley's prestigious Fung Institute with a masters in bioengineering six years ago, claimed his bio on a failed startup company website. DigiTest was a drug testing company that could test for PEDs with a finger prick. Apparently, the market wasn't there to make it viable. Or at least, some people with more money and muscle didn't want blood testing to be that simple.

Cal also located Ted's Linked-In account. The premium upgrade came in handy when researching the background of those he was going to interview, especially on a day like today. He learned that Ted began working at PacLabs three years ago and that he had been involved in DigiTest's failed venture. Nothing else. The guy was as boring as you might expect a lab coat technician to be. His Facebook profile picture was a model strand of DNA. Probably some nerd humor, but it did nothing to shed light on who Ted Simpson really was. Nevertheless, Cal wondered how a Berkley grad ended up in such a drab job. Lead researcher for a failed company to lab tech for a drug testing company? Something didn't add up.

More snooping was needed before Cal headed to the airport for his flight to L.A. It required some drastic measures.

Cal punched in some numbers to his phone and waited for someone to pick up.

"Berkley Alumni Relations. This is Stephanie. How may I help you?"

"Hi, Stephanie. My name is Cal Murphy and I'm a reporter for *The Chronicle*. I want to profile a distinguished graduate from one of your programs and I'm having a hard time locating him. Would you mind looking up his contact information for me?"

The power of the media. Cal had his information in a matter of seconds and started toward the door.

"Murphy! Come here!"

It was Kennedy. Cal hoped he wasn't about to get slammed with some other meaningless assignment when he had a real story to chase.

"What is it?" Cal asked his boss.

"Did you talk to Aretha Banks today?" Kennedy asked in a hushed tone.

"I called her back and left a message. Why?"

"I think there's more to this story and we've got to get on it quick. She's desperate and I don't want any of the TV stations getting wind of this story until we break it. Got it?"

"Got it."

Kennedy slapped Cal on the arm and walked away. Cal let out a sigh of relief and continued toward the newsroom exit.

After Cal made his way down the stairs and to his car in the parking garage, he entered "*69" on his phone and began dialing PacLab's number. Cal had long since learned the value of blocking his number during investigative research.

"PacLabs. My name is Jenny. How may I assist you?"

"Ted Simpson, please," Cal requested as he buckled his seat belt.

"May I ask who's calling?"

"Yes, this Bill Smith from United Lab Suppliers and I wanted to talk to him about a recent order."

"I'm sorry, but Ted went home early sick. Can I take a message?"

Cal hung up.

He grabbed his laptop bag and hurried toward the door. Cal knew time was of the essence or Ted might disappear forever.

* * *

Cal pulled up to the address for Ted's house on Robinhood Drive. It was an older quaint bungalow with a fantastic view of the bay. One of the windows to the left of the front door was open as the drapes flapped in the cool breeze. Someone had to be home.

Cal knocked on the door and called out for his informant.

"Ted! This is Cal. I know you're in there. We need to talk."

There was no reply.

"Come on, Ted. I can keep your name out of this, but I've got to talk to you."

No voice called back, but Cal heard what sounded like some footsteps scuffling across the floor.

"Please, Ted. Open up. This is important."

Finally, the door swung open. A woman dressed in a fluffy pink robe stood in the doorway. A half-lit cigarette clung to lips, serving as an accessory to her yellow curlers attempting to beautify her bedraggled hair. Her gut pooched over what Cal hoped were a long pair of shorts and not boxers, but he didn't stare long enough to figure out which it was.

"Can I help you?" she said in a raspy voice as she squinted at the bright sunshine.

"Yes, I'm Cal Murphy with *The Chronicle* and I'm trying to track down Ted. He does still live here, doesn't he?"

"He told me you might come around looking for him."

"He isn't here?"

"Do I look like Ted's keeper?"

"Frankly, I don't know who you are, but I need to find Ted soon."

"Well, I'm his landlady. He lives in my basement. And he's not here."

"Was he here earlier today?"

"He said you would come looking for him."

"Look, I don't want to take up any more of your time, but I need to know where he went. He might be in danger."

"Here. Take this." The woman handed Cal a key. "It's for a locker at a bowling alley off Van Ness Avenue. His exact words were: 'Don't stall or you might miss it.'"

No. 345. Cal clutched the key and wondered what information might be inside.

"Thanks," Cal said.

Then Cal heard an unfamiliar voice behind him. He also felt a stiff poke in the back. "I'll take that."

Cal relinquished the key and then turned to see a large man wearing a ski mask brooding over him and the landlady.

"If you know what's best for you, you'll keep quiet about this."

Then he fired a shot at the woman and then another at Cal. They both crumpled to the floor.

CHAPTER 8

CHARLES ROBINSON HUFFED AS he straightened the paperclip holder on his mahogany desk. Someone moved the holder. He started to mull who the culprit could have been.

There was a certain order to how he lived, a certain order for how things must be done. Making waves in his pool was not acceptable. And right now, a reporter was doing cannon balls. Robinson needed to calm the waters.

He dialed a number on his phone. A voice on the other end answered the call, but there was no need for introductions.

"Who's that hot shot reporter you hired last year?" Robinson asked.

"Cal Murphy?" the other voice asked.

"Yeah, that's him. Send him down here on assignment to do a big feature on me and our team's rise to prominence. We need some good press."

Robinson hung up. He cared deeply about publicity, but he cared even more about making sure the publicity was good. The notion that all publicity is good publicity was ridiculous at best. Maybe for a rapper or music artist, but not for a businessman trying to build the kind of credibility necessary to create an empire. Robinson wanted to be king of the NFL, but he also wanted to be the king of Forbes 500. He wanted to make Bill Gates look like a pauper in comparison. And Robinson's lust for good publicity was the only reason why he sank any money into the leaky journalism industry. Robinson's narrative would be flawless.

* * *

Miles Kennedy sipped his coffee and stared at the budget for the next day's paper. He cracked his knuckles as he attempted to figure out the new puzzle in front of him. His baseball beat writer just learned that the recent Cy Young Award winning pitcher would be signing with San Francisco the next morning. The front page now needed to undergo a shift. Kennedy surveyed the changing landscape and began thinking how he might navigate it, particularly with all the writers' egos that needed to be assuaged. Each writer held the firm belief that their beat trumped all others—and Kennedy would almost prefer to gouge his eyes out than tell a prima donna reporter that his or her masterpiece would now appear on page three of the sports section instead of the front.

His phone rang. Kennedy grabbed it without moving his eyes from the budget on his desk.

"This is Kennedy."

"I'm so glad I caught you," said the voice on the other end.

"Who is this?"

"It's Kelly Mendoza, from the AP photo bureau in L.A."

"Oh, great. Did we screw up a caption for you?"

"No, no. Nothing like that. I'm trying to find Cal Murphy. Have you heard from him this evening? He isn't answering his cell. It's going straight to voicemail."

"Early this afternoon he told me he was working on a few leads for a story he had, but I haven't heard from him since."

"Do you have any idea where he might be?"

"Sorry, Kelly. I have no idea. But if you find him, please let him know he needs to call me. I've got a new assignment for him."

"OK, thanks."

Kennedy hung up. He dumped his coffee in the trash and began rummaging in his desk drawer for a bottle. Bourbon or Tums—whichever found his hand first would find his stomach next. A new front page was required and now his star reporter was missing.

CHAPTER 9

CAL SQUINTED AT THE LIGHT. His face was flush with the hardwood floor. He didn't immediately remember where he was or what had happened.

"Cal? Are you OK?"

The voice snapped Cal fully awake as he recalled his last few moments of consciousness. A masked man. A key. A gun.

Cal sat up and looked at the woman. It was Ted's landlady. She looked concerned—and afraid.

"I thought we were dead. Who were those guys? What did they want?" she asked.

Still stunned, Cal waited to speak until he pulled the tranquilizer dart out of his neck.

"I have no idea who they were, but they obviously wanted that key," Cal said, turning his pockets inside out and looking around the spot where he had fallen. "It's gone."

Cal then took a quick inventory of all his belongings. Nothing else was missing. He had his keys, his cell phone, his shoes. He didn't possess anything of value other than what was in his pocket and what was on his feet. Obviously, he undervalued the key.

"Have you ever seen Ted hang out with any shady-looking characters?" Cal asked.

"No. I've never seen him hang out with anyone. Nobody ever comes home with him."

"So, he's got no friends?"

"None that I'm aware of. He's absorbed with work and his brother."

"His brother? What's up with him?"

"He's sick. Very sick. I think he has cancer or something like that. But all he does is work and visit his brother."

"Do you know what hospital his brother is at?"

"I have no idea. I barely know his name—Tommy, maybe."

"Well, thanks for your help. Hopefully, I can find Ted soon and clear up what just happened here."

The woman nodded but said nothing, still shaken over the intrusion into her home.

"Look. I know you need to call the cops, but please leave me out of this, OK?" Cal pleaded. "I don't really want to get questioned about all this because I'm trying to keep a low profile in my investigation. If the cops start asking questions, it's going to get around. Word gets out fast."

She agreed to omit Cal from any formal statements.

Cal thanked the woman and left. His head was spinning with possibilities over what was going on. He pulled out his phone and noticed he had a dozen missed calls. *Kelly!*

* * *

Kelly wiped back a few tears streaking down her face. She was starting to get worried. With Cal's penchant for embracing danger, she knew he might be involved in something far more perilous than she first imagined. Cal wasn't one to drop a good lead. She knew that's what made him such a good reporter. It also made a potential future with him seem bleak. But Kelly had her own weakness for a good story, too. Maybe she was overreacting. Maybe she could help.

She brushed a tear away with fingertips and stared at her phone.

"Cal, why do you have to do this to me?" she asked aloud.

Then her phone rang. It was Cal.

"Are you OK?" Kelly asked.

"Yes, Kelly. Thank you! I'm so sorry."

"What happened? I've been trying to get ahold of you all afternoon."

"How does getting knocked out with a tranquilizer gun sound?"

"What?! Are you serious?"

"Yes. I wish I wasn't."

Cal explained what had happened, filling Kelly in on the fine details of the case. He needed a sympathetic ear and a sounding board he could trust. He valued her opinion and wanted to know if his fellow journalist thought the story had any legs.

"This is big, Cal," she finally said.

"You think so?"

"Oh, yes. This might just save your job."

"I was hoping you'd say that. Want to me help me save it?"

"Sure. What do you want me to do?"

Kelly took down Cal's instructions and hung up.

Beneath her breath, Kelly muttered a few curses directed at the imaginary Cal in her car. She wiped away any remnants of tears and then started her car. She had an assignment. They were going to crack this mystery together.

* * *

Cal called Kennedy and and assured him everything was OK, despite Kelly's worrisome phone call. Then Cal received the news—Kennedy was pulling him off the story. Cal protested, but Kennedy stood firm.

"Just drop it, Cal," Kennedy said. "It's a wild goose chase and you know it. Besides, Robinson wants a big feature written on him—and asked you to do it."

"Why would he do that?"

"I don't know. Maybe he likes you. He's good at resurrecting things, you know."

Cal snarled at Kennedy's insinuation and said nothing.

"Look, just go. I know you were going to L.A. tomorrow evening anyway. Now, we'll just reimburse you for the cost of the flight and it's kind of like a free vacation. You can stay down there for a few extra days after the interview. Make it a long Thanksgiving weekend—you know, like most normal people in this country do. Just keep your nose out of that story. Got it?"

Cal mumbled a "yes" and hung up. He didn't mean it.

* * *

Fifteen minutes later, Cal pulled into the Fun Time Bowling Alley parking lot. Fun Time had seen its better days. Tufts of grass spurted out of the cracked pavement. The faded gray stucco building looked as though its owners weren't interested in fighting the tide of new bowling alleys popping up. Paint was peeling off the blue awning that overhung the two double glass doors demarcating the entrance. A few sketchy looking young men took drags of their cigarettes and eyed Cal cautiously as he went inside carrying a small backpack. The interior matched the exterior. Perhaps the purplish carpet appeared fresh and new at some point, but now it had devolved into a grimy maroon that had seen more than its share of foot traffic. The only thing it had going for it was the smell of wood and well-oiled lanes wafting in the air. Though California laws prevented it from being the smoky establishment that it undoubtedly once was, the same characters still likely hung around here. Bikers. Tough guys. Tougher gals. Cocky guys trying to compensate for something with high bowling scores. It was a group of people who wanted to be left alone.

Cal walked up to the desk, staffed by a guy named Bill, according to the name tag sewn onto his shirt. In a matter of moments, Cal spun a story about how his brother's wife wanted to leave a surprise in his locker for his birthday but couldn't sneak down there without her husband knowing. Bill began fumbling for his keys and walked Cal to locker No. 345. He opened it up and told Cal to let him know when he was finished.

Cal sifted through the assorted items in the locker. A dingy bowling shirt. A bag containing a bowling ball. A few stray receipts. Then he checked the shirt pocket that contained a small empty envelope.

It wasn't sealed—and it was empty.

Was this what Ted meant to leave me? Did someone beat me to it?

Cal couldn't be sure.

* * *

Ted pulled his hood over his head and jammed his hands into his jacket pockets. The motel door slammed shut behind him. He had to disappear and he had to pick a place where he was less likely to attract suspicion. The Sunshine Motel met his criteria. Prostitutes, drug dealers, meth addicts, homeless people who scrounged up enough money to sleep on a bed. It's where you went if society had forgotten you—or if you wanted to forget society. This was no way to live.

What Ted once thought was a kind gesture devolved into a tool to manipulate him. If PacLabs wanted something from him—anything from him—one quick threat of removing his brother from the experimental treatment that was keeping him alive made Ted cave every time. He knew he had to comply. He had seen what they were capable of and he wanted out.

He thought he had eluded their suspicion by claiming to be sick as his reason for leaving work early. But the call he received in the late afternoon showed that wasn't the case. They told him to report for work the next day. "You wouldn't want your brother to get hurt, would you?" came the thinly veiled threat.

Reporting meant he was as good as dead. But not reporting meant his brother would likely be also. Who's to say they both weren't already as good as dead? He needed some time to think about his next assignment.

CHAPTER 10

CAL'S RESTLESS NIGHT OF SLEEP mercifully ended when his phone began buzzing.

"Hello?" he mumbled.

"Good morning, Cal," Kelly said cheerily.

"I hope you have a good reason for calling."

"Well, aren't we Mr. Sunshine today?"

Cal grunted.

"OK, maybe I'll call you back after you've had some coffee. I've only spent all night working on these phone records for you."

Cal had almost forgotten the assignment he gave Kelly. He wanted to find out who called Aaron Banks the day he died.

"Oh, Kelly, I'm sorry. It's early and my brain isn't quite working. What did you find?"

A year ago, Kelly told Cal about Oscar Sanders, a co-worker from the IT department who used to moonlight as a hacker for some London newspapers. He never got caught and quit when the newspapers came under serious public ridicule for hacking into celebrities' phones. Oscar was fond of Kelly, who took advantage of that to draw him out of his early hacker retirement.

"We didn't find anything too interesting at first," Kelly said. "He was a creature of habit and seemed to call the same people at regular intervals for the past year. But then on the day he died, we discovered an incoming call from a burner phone. It was the last one he received."

"What's so odd about that?" Cal asked.

"He only started receiving calls from this number nine months ago. And he received only one a month. Not once did he place a call to that number."

"Can you find out who it was that placed the call?"

"Not even Oscar can trace burner phones. That's next to impossible. However, he did manage to find out where the call originated from."

"Oh? Where was that?"

"Near the L.A. Stars' facility."

"Kelly, Aaron Banks played for the Stars. What's so unusual about that?"

"Exactly, Cal. He played for the Stars—and they were using a burner phone. Somebody there didn't want to get linked back to him."

"Good point—and great work, Kelly. We'll see if this is somehow related to PacLabs in any way."

Cal planned the rest of his Thanksgiving weekend with Kelly. He knew she loved working on these types of cases with him. Usually she served as a sounding board, but she had helped him on a few stories in the past. She might be excited to see him this weekend, but he could tell she was anxious to help more with this intriguing story.

* * *

Even though Kennedy directed Cal to stop working on the drug testing story, Cal convinced his editor to let him write a reflective piece on Aaron Banks. Cal thought it was unsympathetic and cruel to give a grieving mother hope that someone would look into her son's death and then renege. While Cal wasn't doing the kind of digging he wanted to, if he unearthed something then he would revisit it with Kennedy.

Cal pulled into Aretha Banks' driveway at 11 a.m. sharp. The

Tuscan style mansion sprawled across the secluded lot in San Francisco's Sea Cliff neighborhood. Pristine landscape fell mostly in the shadows of the three-story structure. To Cal, it was a home that pretended to be from another era but was likely no older than five years based on when Aaron Banks received his new contract with a monster bonus. In his quick research of Aretha Banks, Cal discovered she was a single mother of three kids who worked as a kindergarten teacher. The home was obviously a gift.

Despite the air of pretentiousness the house exuded, it disappeared when Aretha Banks answered the door herself. She invited Cal in.

"Nice place you got here," Cal said, admiring the artwork in the foyer.

"Thank you," Aretha said. "Aaron always promised to take care of me."

"Again, Mrs. Banks. I'm sorry for your loss. All I hear about Aaron is what a wonderful young man he was."

She struggled to hold back her tears before thanking Cal and directing him to the sitting room just off the foyer.

They talked for a few minutes about Aaron's career and about his philanthropy. Aretha warmed to Cal quickly. Cal decided it was time to dive in.

"Now you told my editor that you don't think Aaron committed suicide. Why exactly do you think that?"

Aretha took a deep breath before answering.

"Aaron never once talked about suicide. He was so full of life. I even spoke with him on Sunday night after his game and he was so excited about going to the hospital and visiting those kids. We even made plans for later this week. I was going to fly down to see him on Thanksgiving Day and stay for the game on Sunday."

"Was he depressed?"

"Maybe a little. He hated living in L.A., but he had fallen in love with the kids at St. Mark's Hospital. There wasn't anything he enjoyed more each week than visiting them. He talked more about them than he did his football career."

"What do you think about all these allegations that he failed a drug test and the NFL was going to suspend him?"

"Please," she said indignantly. "Aaron wouldn't eat a candy bar unless it was organic. It took me a year to learn how to prepare raw foods just so I could cook him something he wouldn't turn his nose up at. His only weakness was barbecue. And unless someone was secretly injecting his ribs with performance enhancing drugs, it wasn't getting into his body. Lord knows the team wanted Aaron to use them though."

"What do you mean?"

"Aaron told me the team asked him to use PEDs once. He politely declined. A few weeks later, someone claiming to be associated with the team asked me if I would try and persuade Aaron to use PEDs. They said they were going to cut him if I didn't—and that I would lose my big house. I laughed at him and hung up. This house is paid for and Aaron helped me set up a fund to make sure I'd never run out of money. I know what they are saying is all a bunch of lies."

"So, let's suppose you're right. Let's say that Aaron didn't commit suicide. Who do you think would possibly want to murder him?"

"I have no idea, but I know nothing the team is saying is true. He never had a concussion so I think it's ridiculous that reporters are saying that's the reason he killed himself. I made him bring home copies of his baseline tests, and I took them to a doctor friend of mine to make sure the team wasn't putting him at risk. My friend told me Aaron's results were so low, there's no evidence he ever had even one concussion."

Cal stopped scribbling notes and looked Mrs. Banks in the eyes. "Seriously? You checked on your grown son like that?"

"They never stop being your baby," she said.

"Do you have those reports?"

"Sure do," Mrs. Banks said, sliding a manila folder across the coffee table toward him. "I thought you might want these."

"Thank you very much, Mrs. Banks. I'm not sure what I'll be able to find out, but I'll do my best. I'm going to be at the memorial service next week. And again, I'm sorry for your loss."

Aretha thanked Cal and led him out.

Cal stuffed the folder in his bag and pondered what he had just learned. Mrs. Banks may not have had any idea who killed her son, but Cal did.

CHAPTER 11

THE CHRONICLE OFFICES WERE BUSTLING early Wednesday afternoon. The day before a holiday meant earlier deadlines and plenty of weekend fluff pieces. In a matter of hours, the newsroom would be run by the copy editors and page designers who were lowest on the totem pole. Cal always thought it odd that the most well-read papers of the years were cobbled together by the least experienced. But he wasn't complaining since he fell into the "holiday off" category.

Hardman delivered another wisecrack in poor taste, one more suited for the locker room than the newsroom, but Cal ignored him again. He relished the moment when he was going to rub Hardman's nose in it—though that still seemed far away given the facts Cal had in hand.

Cal sat down at his desk and less than 30 seconds later, his phone rang. It was Kennedy.

"Get in here, Cal. We need to talk."

Cal always hated such invitations. It never resulted in a positive outcome.

Kennedy gestured for Cal to sit down as soon as he entered his office and closed the door behind him. Cal combined the papers strewn over the two guest chairs into one so he could sit down.

"What do you need?" Cal asked.

"How was your interview with Mrs. Banks?"

"I thought it went well. She's obviously still torn up about her son's death, but it was a good interview."

"You're not poking around on this conspiracy story still, are you?"

"Why would you ask that?"

"Look, I'm serious, Cal. I know you and I know the pressure you're feeling. But trust me when I say this—the pressure will get much worse if you go against what I'm asking you to do and drop it. Aaron Banks' memorial is on Tuesday and I want a winning piece for next Wednesday's paper."

"OK, but she told me some stuff today that makes me think Aaron's death was no accident."

"Like what?"

Cal explained to Kennedy about the Stars coercing him to take PEDs and the news about the concussion baselines. It didn't move him.

"So, you've still got a grieving mother who can't accept that her son did drugs and thinks the club is covering something up?"

"Yeah, Kennedy, but there's more to it than that."

"Sounds like she wants to use you to help set up a nice civil lawsuit against the Stars. She's looking for a pay day."

"She's not like that—"

"Of course she is. Who isn't looking for easy money these days? She's playing you."

"Kennedy, do you think the worst of everyone?"

"Do you think the best? Keep thinking like that, Cal, and you're going to get not just burned, but scorched, in this business. We print factual stories, not conjectures and conspiracies. That's what blogs are for. Now keep your nose out of this story or you won't like the outcome."

Kennedy motioned for Cal to leave.

"By the way," Kennedy added, "I got you a press pass for Sunday's Raiders-Stars game. I thought a little insight from

Aaron's teammates might help with your piece on him and the Charles Robinson profile. You'll still be in L.A. on Sunday, right?"

"Yeah, I'll still be there."

Cal returned to his desk questioning his own journalistic sense. His suspicion of others had served him well in the past. But Aaron's death is what seemed more suspicious to him than his mother's tale of an NFL team run amok. Two delicious stories, neither of which had enough facts to be printed.

With one source hiding out and the only other information he had was guess work at best, Cal felt stuck. Not to mention Kennedy was trying to shut him down on this story for some reason. He needed a new lead or some more facts soon.

For good measure, Cal called PacLabs again and asked for Ted. Jenny reported that he was unavailable and wouldn't be so until after the holiday weekend on Monday. Another dead end.

With no Ted to talk to, Cal decided to dig into his past, maybe find out something about him that would shed light on his current behavior. He called the Fung Institute to see if any of Ted's previous professors could be of any help. Cal identified a professor who worked in Ted's field and inquired about Ted. The professor pointed in the direction of Dr. Sandy Jacobs, who served as Cal's mentor in the program.

After introducing himself, Cal asked Dr. Jacobs if he remembers much about Ted Simpson.

"Why? Is he in some sort of trouble?"

"Dr. Jacobs, I'm just a reporter, not a police officer. I'm just trying to find out more about him for a story I'm working on regarding NFL drug testing."

"Drug testing? Now that was Ted's area of expertise. Did you know he developed a blood test for HGH that had nearly a 100% success rate? Worked with a small prick of the finger. It was sheer genius."

"No, I didn't know that."

"Yes, it was part of his thesis work. He and several other classmates tried to make a go of it as a small enterprising company. They tried to sell their test to the NFL, but they claimed it was faulty. That was a lie but I guess that's what happens when you run up against powerful people who would rather discredit you than admit the truth."

"What happened with his classmates?"

"Well, that's what I thought you were calling about—to give me the bad news about Ted."

"Bad news? What do you mean?"

"Ben Sanders, Paul Phillips, and Trevor Wyatt were the three guys who worked with Ted to start DigiTest. They're all dead now."

"All dead? How?"

"It was freaky really. Ben had a heart condition nobody knew about and dropped dead from a heart attack while rock climbing. Paul blew a tire out while driving across the Vallejo Bridge and flipped over the guardrail and into the Carquinez Strait. And Trevor died in a fight at an illegal gambling club in Chinatown. They were all such bright young scientists with promising futures."

Cal asked the obvious follow-up question. "You don't think that's suspicious at all?"

"Maybe a little, but any good scientists knows random occurrences don't make a solid theory. They are all plausible in and of themselves. Ben loved rock climbing. Paul drove across that bridge each day. And Trevor's gambling habit was no secret to those who knew him well. Besides, Ted's still alive."

"For now," Cal muttered.

"Do you think he's in danger?" asked Dr. Jacobs.

"I'm not sure at this point, but he might be. I've been trying to contact him for this story I'm working on and he claims to be out sick. But his landlady hasn't seen him in a couple of days."

"I hope he's OK," Dr. Jacobs added. His concern seemed genuine to Cal.

"Is there anything else about DigiTest that you think would be helpful?"

"Not really. Ben was the real financial brains behind the venture. Once he died and then the other two within the next six months, Cal had to shut it down. He was just clueless about how to proceed as a profitable business. What is it he's doing these days?"

"He's a lab tech at PacLabs."

"A lab tech!? Are you serious? When you find him, tell him to call me so I can help him find suitable employment for someone of his intellect."

Cal thanked Dr. Jacobs and hung up.

Three young scientists dead in six months? An NFL player commits suicide while still in his prime? A lab fixing drug tests of NFL players? Cal began to see a tapestry forming. He just needed to find the common thread.

CHAPTER 12

LATER THAT EVENING, CAL caught his flight for L.A. As much as he wanted to plumb the depths of his front-page scandal story, Cal let his mind wander toward much more peaceful thoughts, thoughts about Kelly. He still hoped that maybe they would both land in the same city—or that one of them would be willing to lay down their journalistic pursuits. But he knew the latter would never happen. His affection for Kelly was rivaled only by his passion for journalism. He knew she felt the same way. For now, this short-distance-long-weekend relationship worked.

But Cal wanted it all—the girl and the job. If forced to admit the truth, Cal might also acknowledge that Kelly always seemed to fill the gaps in his story with piercing questions. He needed her—and for plenty of reasons.

When he landed, Kelly picked him up and drove back to her gated apartment. She had moved two weeks before and was eager to show Cal her new place.

"A gate? You're moving up in the world," Cal chided her.

"OK, I know it's crazy, but I wanted to live closer to work and this was the best neighborhood for it. It's not the best part of town, I know. So, that's why there's a gate."

Cal loved ribbing Kelly, especially about things like being in a high brow apartment complex. She hated pretentiousness, which made it all the more fun for Cal to tease her about it.

After dinner, they caught up on friends, co-workers, and potential locations they could vacation together in the summer. But Cal finally directed the conversation where he wanted it to go all night.

"I spoke with one of Ted's old professors today," Cal said.

"Cal! I thought we weren't supposed to talk about work, remember?"

"I know, I know. But I thought you might be able to help me figure out some gaps in my investigation."

"Fine. Go ahead." She rolled her eyes, but Cal could tell it was feigned at best.

He caught Kelly up to speed on all the findings from his research and conversation with Dr. Jacobs. She was as convinced as Cal that somehow everything was connected.

"The motivation for why the Stars would do this is disturbing," Kelly said after thinking for a few minutes. "Suppose Mrs. Banks' story is true. Why would the Stars try to convince Aaron Banks to take PEDs? And why would they lie about him having symptoms from a concussion? It doesn't make sense."

Just as Cal began to respond, a brick broke through the window, sending shards of glass flying about the room. It almost hit Cal, who was sitting on the floor. Kelly began screaming as she stood on the couch against the far wall. Tires squealed; whoever it was that delivered the brick didn't want to be seen or caught.

Cal froze, surrounded by a sea of splintered glass. Before he moved, he asked Kelly if she was working on anything that would generate such a response. Then he reached for the brick, which had a note attached to it by a rubber band.

Stop poking your nose where it doesn't belong ... for you and your sweetheart's sake

Cal shuddered. Someone followed him. How else would they know where he was? And who was "they" anyway? The lab? Ted Simpson? The Stars? It was hard to know who didn't want him sticking his nose in their business.

Cal calmed Kelly down before picking her up and carrying her to safe ground in the kitchen. He then called the police and reported the vandalism. Kelly wasn't in any mood to ponder who did this to her apartment or why. She expressed that she felt violated. Cal struggled to bite his lip and discuss the case no more with her. Nevertheless, his mind raced with possibilities.

About an hour after Cal called the police, they finally showed up. Lt. Fisk, one of the two responders, asked all the questions. Cal sensed the guy wasn't happy about working on the eve of a holiday. He filled out a report and had Cal sign it, offering no idea of when they might be able to track the perpetrator down. Nor did he look interested. He gave Kelly a case number and told her to call their precinct on Monday to obtain a report for insurance if she needed it.

Cal cleaned up the glass, left to his own thoughts. At least he had something to be thankful for—neither he nor Kelly got hurt.

* * *

Thanksgiving Day proved to be uneventful on the investigative front. Cal promised not to talk about the case or what happened the night before. Instead, they had a big meal with some of Kelly's work friends before hiking around nearby Sturtevant Falls.

They returned home in time to catch most of the late Thanksgiving Day game between the Giants and the Cowboys. Cal wasn't a fan of either team, but he wasn't about to pass up an American tradition. He convinced Kelly to join him.

The game didn't offer much in the way of exciting plays or gripping theater. Most of the dead air was filled by the announcers speculating on the future of the Cowboys' coaching staff, which seemed like a new tradition that had emerged in recent years. Kelly grew bored with the game, escaping into a copy of *Sunset* magazine.

Cal almost turned the game off before the halftime teaser arrested his attention.

"Tonight during our halftime report, we'll take a look back at the career of Aaron Banks, look at today's earlier games, and get a fascinating report from Molly Andrews on sports concussions and mental illness."

Cal wondered how she could pull such a report together so fast for a prime time broadcast. He considered such a report to be in poor taste as it was being done so close to Aaron's death—and the on the heels of a tribute to him, no less. But this was television. If newspapers moved at the speed of Mach 1, television moved at the speed of light. It was real time reporting, reporting that often played fast and loose with the facts. Cal remained on the couch with a smug look on his face. He was glad he wasn't a television reporter and that he earned his jobs on merit, not cleavage and good looks.

Riveted to the screen, Cal watched the tribute and took sharp mental notes. Three teammates talked about how great of a person Aaron Banks was and what a tragedy it was that he took his own life. They all hinted that maybe there was something else going on, but didn't directly say. What they didn't say and who they didn't interview made Cal curious.

He knew from covering the Seahawks' beat before moving to San Francisco that NFL players typically hung out with other players who played on the same side of the ball. Offensive players hung out with other offensive players. Defensive players did the same. And when it came to the closest relationships among the players, they usually were found among players who played the same type position. Offensive linemen hung out with other offensive linemen. Defensive backs went out to dinner with each other regularly. They were like mini fraternities.

The tribute piece on Aaron Banks only included one offensive player—an offensive lineman—and two linebackers from the defense.

Then came Molly's sterling report. She interviewed brain surgeons who warned of the dangers of concussion and how it can change the chemical makeup of the brain. She followed up the medical portion of her report by sharing several anecdotes about players who committed suicide and how their autopsies showed severe brain damage. The camera panned in on her to frame her face—along with her cleavage—so she could deliver her powerful closing remarks about "losing another great player at far too young an age in Aaron Banks." The two broadcasters echoed Molly's sentiments exactly, saying nothing of the story, which seemed as out of place as a bikini in the arctic. Some producer got wrapped up in the moment and was trying to make some connection to current events with the report. Cal was still glad he had time to research his stories instead of shoving them out there like a half-baked casserole.

He pulled out his phone and made some notes. He was going to interview more than Charles Robinson tomorrow. And he needed Kelly's help.

CHAPTER 13

CAL WOKE UP EARLY Friday morning and got ready for the day. He showered and made Kelly breakfast. It was a gesture with mixed motives, half hoping to impress her with his eggs benedict, half serving as a bribe to coerce her to help him. His plan worked. Then he proceeded to go over the more important plan—the one that was going to get him a front-page blockbuster story and save his job.

Despite the long holiday weekend, the Stars' business office was bustling as usual when Cal and Kelly arrived. The office was a modest four-story building adjacent to the Stars' practice facility. The plain stucco structure stood in stark contrast to the team's flashy personality. If it weren't for the monument topped with a golden star, it could have served as a bank or a group of doctors' offices.

Cal suggested they enter the building separately so they wouldn't raise any suspicion. He instructed Kelly to wait at least 15 minutes since he had no idea how long Robinson would keep him waiting.

Cal strode up to the receptionist's desk and explained his appointment. The receptionist took down his name, gave him a visitor's badge and phoned Robinson's assistant. It would be a five-minute wait. Of course it would be a wait, Cal thought. It's a time-honored tradition for people of power to make the lessers waste time. Everyone did it, but it still irked Cal.

The wait extended to ten minutes until an Asian woman with tightly-cropped, shoulder-length dark hair opened a door that led into the rest of the building. She asked Cal to follow her back to meet Robinson.

She led Cal down a long corridor filled with framed photos of L.A. Stars players in action. Many of the other NFL team offices Cal had visited hung their franchise's defining moment—a Super Bowl victory, a miraculous win, a division title. The Stars had none of these yet, but Robinson seemed like a man who was determined to change that at all costs, especially if Ted's allegations were true.

The woman passed by what was her desk with the nameplate of Kiaria Zhou. Everything on her desk appeared ordered, down to the nametags attached to her stapler and paper clip holder. She instructed Cal to wait for a moment while she notified Robinson he was ready to be seen. It gave Cal time to read the screen saver quote by Confucius on her computer terminal: "The perfecting of one's self is the fundamental base of all progress and all moral development."

After a brief exchange with Robinson, she motioned for Cal to enter Robinson's office. Robinson remained seated as Cal entered the room, a room so orderly that Cal thought perhaps everything might be glued in place.

"Thank you for coming down here on a holiday weekend, Mr. Murphy," Robinson said, gesturing for Cal to sit in one of the chairs facing his desk.

Cal nodded. "Not a problem, Mr. Robinson."

"No, please call me Charles."

The invitation to call Robinson by his first name took Cal aback for a moment. Maybe Robinson wasn't the pretentious, power-hungry perfectionist he believed him to be.

"OK, Charles," Cal said eyeing a picture on Robinson's desk. He picked it up and showed it to Robinson. "Is this your son?"

"My son-in-law, Carlton, with my daughter, Vienna."

"Nice looking kids. I think—"

"Let's cut the small talk," Robinson interrupted. "I've got a busy schedule and you've got to fill up some space on the front page about how incredible I am for one of the twelve newspapers I own. So, let's get started, shall we?"

Nope. Cal's first instincts were right. So much for warming up the interview subject.

Cal dove in with his first question: "So, Charles, can you tell me about your first NFL game experience and how that impacted you?"

And away the interview went.

* * *

Kelly tapped her finger on her cell phone, checking it nervously. Cal said to wait at least fifteen minutes, but she decided to wait nineteen. A random number, but it was her lucky number. At 10:19, she got out of her car and headed for the entrance to the Stars' office building.

The same receptionist who greeted Kelly put her through the same routine as Cal, inquiring about the nature of her visit.

"I'm Kelly Mendoza from the Associated Press and I'm here to meet Brandon Freely from the AV department," she said.

The receptionist dialed a number and told Kelly to have a seat because Brandon would be a few moments.

Through her work at the AP bureau, Kelly met Brandon. He often gave Kelly photos when she went looking for an action shot of a certain player but the bureau's photos weren't the required quality. Brandon oversaw a team of talented photographers, videographers and producers who captured still photos and video images for the Stars each week. Before working for the Stars, Brandon was a successful Hollywood producer. But he got burnt out from the rugged production schedules movie making demanded and sought a more regular schedule. The Stars snapped him up, and Brandon's video productions aired at the stadium during home games became a regular topic of conversation on local Monday morning sports talk shows. His following was cult-like as there were at least a dozen blogs who posted and critiqued Brandon's videos after each game.

Brandon finally came through the door and exchanged pleasantries with Kelly before leading her toward his office.

"I can't believe it has taken me this long to actually come down here and see where all the magic happens," Kelly said.

"You're too kind, Kelly. Right this way."

Brandon led her through a few more doors and hallways before finally arriving at the AV office. It was a large room devoid of windows and dotted with cubicles. A few stations had large flat-screen monitors as young employees appeared to be tweaking and editing video footage. He gave Kelly a quick tour before taking her to his office, the only one in the room with a door.

"So, what prompted this tour?" Brandon asked.

"Oh, it's Thanksgiving weekend and I didn't have to work, so I thought it might be nice to visit. I never have time to do this stuff when I'm scheduled to work."

Brandon smiled and nodded knowingly.

"So would you like to see the rest of the facility?" he asked.

"Sure."

It was the real reason Kelly visited in the first place.

* * *

Cal found his interview with Robinson enlightening. He read that Robinson grew up poor, but he never realized just how poor. Robinson's mother raised him and his three siblings by herself after her husband died in a bar room fight one night. Robinson said it was just as well since his father beat the entire family on a regular basis. A toothpaste cap left off or an improperly folded newspaper were acts that riled up Robinson's father and led to a beating.

As a teenager, Robinson grew tired of living impoverished and vowed to become rich. He took advantage of financial aid, went to the University of Southern Cal, and joined a fraternity. He refused to reveal his major to Cal, insisting that the most important thing about the college experience is learning how to network. Robinson then explained how he leveraged his network to help him get ahead, sharing how a few key relationships helped him meet the integral people who launched his business career.

After Cal had sufficient fodder to create a portrait of Robinson for the article, Robinson concluded by saying his goals in life had changed. He now wanted to be filthy rich so he could be more philanthropic when he eventually retired. It was a goal Robinson was on his way to achieving, a goal that he made sound noble.

In writing his article, Cal would present Robinson in the best light possible, especially since he owned the media conglomerate that ran *The Chronicle*. But Cal saw the true Robinson—and now he had no doubt that Robinson was so driven, he would do anything to win. Anything.

Cal checked his watch as he got up to leave. He dragged the interview out fifteen minutes longer than he was scheduled for. Wanting to make the most of his visit to the Stars' office, he then swung by the media relations office to pick up his press credential for Sunday's game.

Cal hoped Kelly pulled it off. He could wait to find out what she learned.

But when he arrived at his car, Kelly wasn't there.

CHAPTER 14

AFTER A LONG LAZY TOUR with Brandon, Kelly asked to use the restroom. He gave her directions and returned to his office.

Kelly crept past the restrooms and up a flight of stairs at the end of the hall. She had swiped an access card from a vacant interns' desk in order to gain access to the medical records room she spotted during the tour. No one was in the hall.

She made her way down to the hall and waved her card in front of the access panel. The door clicked and she opened it. While on the tour, Brandon had opened the door and showed her the room. She noted the organization of the filing system. It came in handy now as she needed to move fast to find Aaron Banks' medical records.

It didn't take long before she found his folder and began taking pictures with her camera phone. It was a thick file, but she raced through as many pertinent documents as she could find before returning the folder and slipping out of the room.

She nearly reached the foot of the stairs before she heard a voice shouting in her direction.

"Hey! What are you doing young lady?"

Kelly spun around to see a portly gentlemen wearing a light blue shirt with dark pants. He also carried a stick and wore a holster with a gun. *A security guard.*

"I was looking for the restroom and got turned around," Kelly stammered.

The guard glared at her, unsure if her response was honest. Then Kelly made sad eyes, which gave her the appearance of being innocent. It was enough to convince the security guard.

"The second floor is off limits to unaccompanied visitors. The bathrooms on the first floor are next to the stairwell just below us."

"Thank you," Kelly said before scampering down the stairs.

She returned to Brandon's office to thank him for the tour. He ushered her out through the front doors.

* * *

While waiting for Kelly, Cal wasted no time. He put in a request to interview the coroner who examined Aaron Banks' body. It was a lead worth exploring.

He then turned the radio on and began listening to sports talk radio. Banks died on Monday, but the hot topic was still concussions and player safety. KSPN's Mark Willard was interviewing Buck Mason, president and CEO of Head Gear.

"Buck, your company has been searching for ways to address this issue in high impact sports and from what I understand you've made some technological breakthroughs. Tell us about that."

"Sure, Mark. We've done extensive testing of our helmets with a handful of NFL teams as well as with college, high school and recreational teams. And the results are pretty exciting. Our helmets won't prevent concussions entirely, but players who wore our helmets reduced the likelihood of getting a concussion by ninety-eight percent."

"Wow, Buck. That's incredible."

"It really is. And while I know there are plenty of parents out there who are hesitant to let their kids play football these days, our innovation goes beyond the NFL and college level. This spring, our new line of helmets will be available for youth and high school teams as well. We're excited about our commitment to making football as safe as possible."

"This is great news, especially in light of the recent tragedies around the NFL related to head injuries. And for all your investors out there,

Head Gear will have a public offering in a couple of weeks. I'm not a financial advisor, but this company seems like a no-brainer—no pun intended."

Cal rolled his eyes. The idea that a study could quantify the amount of reduction in potential concussions was laughable. It was some pseudo-science hocus-pocus that was undoubtedly going to make Buck Mason a rich man. And if he was a smart man, he'd sell his share and retire before the lawsuits started flooding in the minute a kid suffered a concussion wearing one of their helmets.

Cal was checking his watch when Kelly climbed into the passenger side seat; she sighed.

"That took you long enough. I was starting to get worried. Did you get the files?"

"Yes—and you're not going to believe what I found," Kelly said.

Cal's phone started buzzing.

"Hang on. I want to hear all about it."

Cal answered his phone. "Hey, Kennedy. How are you?"

"Not good, Cal."

"Why? What's going on?"

"I told you to drop it with the Aaron Banks' conspiracy theory. Just go down to L.A., write a puff piece on Robinson and get back for Banks' memorial. This was your chance to get back in good graces with upper management. But you couldn't leave it alone, could you?"

"What are you talking about?"

"You know what I'm talking about—the request to interview Banks' coroner."

"How did you know about that? I just made that request like fifteen minutes ago. Besides, what's wrong with that?"

"Never mind how I know about it. I told you to drop it— that's what's wrong with it. And you didn't. And now you're fired."

"Fired?! What?"

Cal watched Kelly's eyes grew wide as she went slack-jawed from hearing one side of his conversation.

"Yeah, you heard me, Cal. Fired," Kennedy said. "I'm not excited about it and I hate to let you go, but this decision came over my head. Just promise me next time you'll listen to your editor when he says stop, OK?"

Cal tried to apologize, searching for the right words. He wanted to convince Kennedy he was right for continuing to investigate Aaron Banks' death and the possible link to PacLabs, but it would be a futile effort. Kennedy didn't fire him. Someone high above Kennedy wanted him gone.

And that someone didn't like Cal snooping around when there was something to hide.

CHAPTER 15

TED SIMPSON DESPISED THE FACT that he was in this situation. Life had dealt him a rotten hand yet he kept drawing bad cards. Two dead parents, a dying brother, a once-promising career. Not to mention that his only friends were those he met online in role play games after all his real friends died. Maybe it was better that way, living in some virtual reality. The real one he lived in certainly wasn't worth delving into. He couldn't even get a date with PacLabs' scatter-brained receptionist.

His phone rang.

"Yeah," he answered.

"So, have you decided what you're going to do?" said the voice on the other end.

"I'll do it."

Ted hung up. He felt nauseous. He thought maybe this was it, the one opportunity to turn around his pathetic life. It would assure his brother's safety and he could escape somewhere, anywhere. He could start over, lay down a winning hand and reclaim some of his lost riches. He could stomach the assignment if it meant he could make all his troubles vanish. It would be worth it. But his nausea remained.

* * *

The news of Cal's firing cast a dour mood over he and Kelly. It was challenging enough to gather enough information and sources to write a story of this magnitude for an editor who trusted you and with all the resources a large media conglomerate could offer. But without an editor? Or a platform to write it for? Cal felt this story slipping away into the abyss.

Cal told Kelly he didn't want to talk. She remained quiet for the rest of the ride back to her apartment before breaking the silence.

"I'm sorry, Cal," she said. "I know this can't be easy, especially when you're just doing your job."

"I really thought Kennedy had my back—but it's clear someone wants me shut down."

"There's only one thing to do then," Kelly said.

"Drink?"

Kelly laughed. "No. We're going to keep doing exactly what they don't want us to. We're going to keep digging."

"So, what did you find at the Stars' facility?" Cal asked, obviously in agreement with Kelly's counter suggestion.

"You're going to want to take a look at this."

Kelly plugged her iPhone into her desktop computer and began downloading the pictures. She began opening them up one by one.

"What are we looking at here?" Cal asked.

"These are Aaron Banks' team medical records. There were two files on him, almost identical with the exception of the concussion baseline tests."

Kelly pecked away on the keyboard and called up two files with the same date from the current year. One showed the evidence of a concussion, the other didn't. Then she called up two files with the identical dates from the previous year. The same alterations were shown.

"These records have been tampered with. It's clear that someone wanted Aaron Banks' death to appear as it were concussion related."

Kelly's last statement hung in the air. A million questions

flooded Cal's mind. Who? Why? Did Aaron Banks really commit suicide? If so, why make it look like it was concussion related? If not, who did kill him? And how on earth was this related to the falsified drug tests Ted Simpson gave him? The number of potential rabbit trails was enough to drive him mad.

Cal said nothing as he pondered the best course of action.

"So what do you think we should do, Cal?" Kelly asked.

"I think we should call Aretha Banks," he said. "And call your cousin, the coroner. We need an independent autopsy report on Aaron."

They both swung into action, dialing away on their phones. This course of action required fast talking to get Mrs. Banks to agree to have her son's body examined again—and to get Kelly's cousin to fly from small town Idaho to San Francisco to inspect it.

Both succeeded in their missions. On Tuesday, Mrs. Banks was holding a closed casket memorial service anyway and nobody would know that his body wasn't there. And Kelly's cousin could do an independent examination on Wednesday morning.

They spent the rest of the day writing out notes and drawing up plausible theories with a list of suspects and motives. The oddities around the case, as well as the attempted cover-up, made Cal far beyond suspicious. He was convinced someone—a someone named Charles Robinson—was benefitting from Aaron Banks' death, he just couldn't figure out who. Cal had even followed the money, but he couldn't find a way to link it to the Stars' owner.

* * *

By 10:30, Cal was tired and ready to go to bed. He was brushing his teeth when there was a loud knock on Kelly's door.

Cal went to the door but didn't see anyone as he looked through the peep hole. He opened the door anyway to make sure. Just as he was about to close the door, he noticed a yellow sticky note on the door that said, "We warned you to drop it."

"Who is it, Cal?" Kelly called from the kitchen where she was getting a drink of water.

Cal lied. "Nobody. I thought I heard a knock."

Just as Cal began to close the door, an explosion rocked the apartment and the nearby streets. For a moment, Cal thought it was an earthquake, but then he saw the fire and smoke plumes filling up the L.A. night sky.

Kelly screamed as she ran to the door.

She screamed louder when she recognized the target of the explosions. Flames engulfed her car. For the second straight night, someone targeted Kelly and Cal. The message had been received. Cal wondered what the next message might be.

It was obvious that he was on the right trail, but he started to wonder if it was worth losing his life over. Or worse yet— losing Kelly.

CHAPTER 16

AFTER ANOTHER LONG NIGHT of dealing with LAPD over Kelly's exploding car and her frazzled emotional state, Saturday morning brought more bad news. Cal was barely conscious when his phone buzzed. The caller ID was blocked.

"Hello?" Cal grumbled.

"Hey, Cal. We need to talk," said the caller.

"Who is this? Are you are aware that it's seven o'clock on a Saturday morning?"

"This is Ted Simpson, Cal. And, yes, I'm fully aware of what time it is."

Cal sat straight up in bed. He was wide awake now.

"What do we need to talk about, Ted?" he asked.

"It's about those papers I gave you."

"What about them?"

"They're fakes. I was just trying to get back at PacLabs for some stuff recently and I went about it the wrong way."

"What?!" Cal asked. His rage was growing. "I have half a mind to find you and punch you in the face, you little weasel. Do you realize what following your little lead has cost me? I have no job now, Ted. I got fired, thanks to your little stunt."

"You got fired? I'm sorry to hear that."

"Yeah, I got fired, no thanks to you. The next time you're ticked off at your employer file a complaint with the HR department. Don't concoct some lie."

Cal continued with more questions.

"What about your little bowling alley locker stunt? Was that fake, too?"

"Yes, Cal. I was just trying to make it more believable for you."

"Did you shoot me and your landlady with a tranquilizer too?"

"I'm really sorry about that."

Cal noted Ted's answer was apologetic—and evasive. He hadn't admitted to shooting them with a tranquilizer, but certainly something had gone awry for the whistleblower. Cal grew more miffed by the moment. He finally delivered clear instructions to Ted before ending the call.

"I don't know what sick little game you've been playing. I'm not even sure I'll ever believe anything out of your mouth ever again. But just to be sure I don't have to figure out if you're telling the truth or not, don't ever call me again. Do you understand?"

Cal didn't wait around for an answer as he hung up.

Kelly, who was up brewing some coffee, heard Cal's side of the conversation and his raised voice. She burst into the room and wanted to know more details immediately.

"He made it all up?" she asked.

"That's what he said. I can't believe this!"

Cal let out a scream in frustration. Hunches motivated by desperation were never good ones. They cost many a good journalists their jobs. "Actionable facts" is what his first editor Guy Thompson used to call them. "If you don't have actionable facts, you don't have a story," he used to tell Cal.

But no matter how frustrated Cal was with Ted, he *did* have actionable facts. Something was clearly fishy with the way the Stars handled the announcement of Aaron Banks' death and the facts surrounding it. At least Ted put him on a path that might result in some type of cover-up story—and maybe even a murder investigation.

Cal still wasn't convinced Ted was telling the truth about the documents being fake.

* * *

The early morning phone call frazzled Cal, but it made him more determined than ever to dig up the truth around Aaron Banks' death. If he ignored Ted's fake drug tests, what did he have? A dead NFL player who was meticulous about what he put in his body. Forged medical documents by the team showing Banks had concussions when he didn't. A quick autopsy. A shoddy police investigation, which seemed far too quick to rule Aaron's death a suicide.

Cal still needed to find the thread that tied it all together.

After breakfast, Cal devised a research plan as Kelly secured a rental car. He would take Charles Robinson and Kelly would take a closer look at the medical records.

Cal began scouring the Internet for more about the Stars' owner, something that would give him motivation to do what he was doing. For more than two hours, he pored over articles and documents about Robinson. Nothing brought clarity.

During his interview with Robinson, Cal learned that the Stars' owner grew his wealth through a series of savvy investments and good fortune. For years he grew his wealth slowly through safe investments. Then in 1997, he invested in a tech startup that made him a multi-millionaire at the age of 48. From there his wealth soared. It seemed like Robinson could do no wrong.

His string of good luck seemed uncanny. In some of the earlier stories on Robinson in business magazines, Cal read how if there were two companies with similar ideas, Robinson always managed to pick the successful one. Small companies, big companies. It didn't matter. Robinson always guessed right.

Many of the companies Robinson owned controlling interest in were listed on the C.R. Enterprises website. With *The*

Chronicle among the media outlets listed, Cal didn't have to guess how he lost his job. But Cal could find no direct link.

Kelly wasn't having much luck either. They decided to commiserate over lunch in the kitchen. Cal made a couple of club sandwiches and grilled them to golden brown perfection. He didn't mind the break from the mind-numbing research. He didn't mind the company either.

After some small talk, Kelly asked the question burning in her mind.

"What are you going to do, Cal?"

"What do you mean?"

"I mean about your job."

Cal thought for a few moments. "Maybe I'll move here."

"Really? L.A.?"

"It's not my first choice based on geography, but you're here. I may not have a job as a reporter since Robinson owns practically every paper in this city, but at least we can be together."

Kelly smiled at Cal. He knew it was the one silver lining in the midst of his career crisis. They had always made a good journalism team. He thought they would make a good team period.

He got up and walked around the table to give Kelly a kiss. He considered himself to be tough, someone who had mastered his emotions. But right now he wanted a hug. He *needed* a hug. Kelly was more than happy to give it to him.

Cal's phone buzzed. It was a text from one of *The Chronicle's* photographers, Mike Gregory.

Sorry, Cal. I caught Hardman snooping around my desk. I couldn't stop him.

Cal replied,

What are you talking about?

The response came back immediately.

Turn on ESPN.

Cal scrambled to the television remote and turned on the TV, flipping furiously to ESPN. Two talking heads were debating the Stars' chances of winning the division. At the bottom of the screen, the reason for the debate scrolled:

SF Chronicle report: L.A. Stars QB Isaiah Smith suspended for failed drug test, according to league sources

Cal let out a string of expletives that sent Kelly scurrying to join him in the living room.

"What is it?"

"That jerk Hardman stole my story!"

CHAPTER 17

CAL DIALED GREGORY'S NUMBER. He needed to know exactly how this went down and why Kennedy chose to print the story.

"Look, Hardman came snooping around my desk and asked what hot tip you had," Gregory explained. "I told him it wasn't any of his business. Well, apparently one of the interns saw us talking and in an effort to get on the side of our big shot columnist, he grabbed the two files off my desktop during lunch yesterday and emailed them to Hardman."

"I'm gonna kill him!" Cal interjected.

"Calm down and let me finish," Gregory said. "So from what I gather, he faxed a copy of the failed drug test to the league office, they called the lab and confirmed it was authentic. They made up some story about how they didn't release it because the Stars were dealing with so much after the loss of Aaron Banks."

Cal was hot. "The only reason they released it is because someone called them on it. PacLabs isn't some beacon of empathy. Besides, they had no problem releasing Banks' failed drug test."

"Apparently, Hardman had enough to run with the story and Kennedy had no choice."

"I can't believe he poached my story. He's a two-bit hack."

"Well, he's a two-bit hack with a Pulitzer—and a job."

Cal was getting agitated. "That's below the belt."

"I'm not trying to be mean, Cal. I'm just saying he's ruthless. That's how he got where he is. It certainly wasn't with his winning personality."

"That's for sure. Thanks for the heads up. Do you still have the thumb drive?"

"Oh, yeah. And I've made a backup copy, too. They're not going to take this from me."

"Would you mind working your magic on those files and sending them all over to my personal email account? I'm still working on the real story here."

"There's more?"

"There's a mountain of more. I just need more sources to put it all together along with a few common threads."

"Cool. Not to sound like a jerk, but have you thought about where you're going to get it published?"

"I'm not sure yet. No paper in California will run it, but last I checked he doesn't own *The New York Times* or ESPN. I'm sure one of them will be proud to run this story."

"Well, good luck, Cal. And I'm sorry again about everything."

"No worries. Just slug Hardman for me the next time you see him and tell him it's from me. I know he only wrote that story because he's a Raiders homer and they play the Stars tomorrow."

"I'd be honored to slug Hardman for you."

Cal said good-bye and hung up. He was more puzzled than ever. Ted's call this morning was meant to throw him off track. If that was Ted at all? He'd only spoken with who he thought was Ted in a coffee shop several days ago. But the informant spoke with a husky whisper, disguising his true voice. Maybe Ted didn't call him at all this morning. Maybe it was someone trying to throw him off the pace or make him distrust Ted.

Cal tried to make sense of it all with Kelly as he relayed

what had happened in the office. She seemed just as confused as Cal.

"Are you still planning on going to the game tomorrow?" Kelly asked.

"You bet. You think you can get a photo pass?"

"Sure. What are you thinking?"

"I'm not sure how welcome I'll be there, but I've got another assignment for you. We're going to find the crack in this case."

CHAPTER 18

FOR THE REMAINDER OF SATURDAY, Cal and Kelly split up. The idea that Ted had actually told him the truth made him wonder about the tact of his investigation. Charles Robinson had likely given the order to fire him, making Cal wonder if perhaps the interview was less about Robinson and more about him. Such motives were vital in solving any mysteries, if there were any. He needed more background on Aaron Banks.

Cal set up an early dinner meeting with Aaron Banks' agent Bobby Franklin at Jackson's BBQ and sent Kelly to visit St. Mark's Hospital. Franklin was the person who knew Aaron best off the field, and St. Mark's was the place where Aaron spent most of his free time away from football. They could also help reconstruct the last few hours of his life.

Jackson's BBQ was legendary in Los Angeles. Started by a two aspiring actors from South Carolina whose careers never panned out, Jackson's quickly gained a reputation as one of the stars' favorite haunts. What the warehouse-style building lacked in decadence, it apparently made up for with flavorful food. Riveted metal siding and dark-coated cement floors housed wooden benches and picnic tables. The walls were lined with stars from every Hollywood galaxy—movies, television, music. Jackson's boasted more about its food than its clientele, but it was clear they were proud of both. According to Franklin, it was Aaron's favorite restaurant.

Franklin, dressed in a power suit with a red tie, was already sitting in a booth when Cal arrived. As a former NFL tight end for several years before retiring early due to an injury and becoming an agent, Franklin's large frame was imposing. His hand swallowed Cal's as they officially met. They exchanged pleasantries before Cal began probing.

"So, what happened on the day Aaron died?" Cal asked. "I heard he had just finished volunteering at the hospital before he committed suicide."

"Yes, God rest his soul. Right before Aaron left the hospital that morning, he called me."

"What did you talk about?"

"His career. He had just found out the Stars were going to release him at the end of the season."

"So he was going to be a free agent. Wouldn't he be able to get a bigger payday with a new contract?"

"Sure. I would've had half a dozen teams beating down the door to sign a blue collar running back like Aaron Banks. He did all the little things coaches love without the ball and he knew how to find the end zone when he was with it. But he didn't want to leave. I think he loved volunteering at the hospital more than he did playing football."

A waitress interrupted their conversation to take their orders. Cal chose the Elvis platter—Memphis-style pulled pork with baked beans and fries. Franklin ordered the Sweet Home Alabama plate, which consisted of nothing but ribs and a loaf of white bread.

"So, how did your conversation go?" Cal continued.

"I told him and he got pretty angry," Franklin said. "Then another call came and he told me he would meet me here in a few minutes, but he never showed."

"Did you know he was using PEDs?"

"Yes, he told me a few weeks before. I told him that wasn't a good idea, but he said that it was foolproof and he wouldn't get caught. I was shocked, to tell you the truth. Aaron was not the kind of guy who used PEDs. When I asked him why he was doing it, he said that someone affiliated with the organization told him if he didn't they were going to release him. I think he only did it because he wanted to stay here in L.A. And I think that's why he got so angry when I told him the Stars were releasing him. He had gone against his own principles just to stay here, doing whatever they asked and now he was getting tossed aside. He wasn't quite the player he used to be, but it's hard for guys not to take that stuff personally."

"So you don't think that was enough to drive Aaron to kill himself?" Cal asked.

"Maybe. He was a pretty happy guy, a guy who loved what playing football afforded him. He wanted to make a difference in people's lives. But he was lonely and depressed at times. I knew he was capable of killing himself, but I never thought he would actually do it. It's still shocking."

"I'm assuming the police interviewed you. Did you tell them this?"

"Yeah, they interviewed me. They just wanted me to confirm what they said they already knew. They had the facts and they said that he killed himself. They simply wanted to know what we talked about before he allegedly shot himself."

"I did some digging too, and I found out that the last number that called him came from a burner phone that had called once a month for the past nine months. Any idea who it might have been?"

"Maybe his supplier," Franklin suggested. "That's still rather odd. Aaron didn't run with any shady people."

The waitress brought them their food, topped off their drinks and winked at Franklin.

"Do you think his supplier could have done this?" Cal asked between bites.

"I don't know," Franklin said. "Most suppliers I know are

sketchy, but they aren't assassins. I would be shocked if they could pull this off."

"So, essentially, you're saying someone affiliated with the Stars' organization was supplying Aaron with illegal PEDs but you don't think they could've actually killed him?"

"Yes.Perhaps he killed himself over the news that the team wanted to trade him. It's just so bizarre."

"Well, finding enough evidence to claim the someone else killed him has proven to be an enormous task."

"I still can't believe he's gone. He had such a bright future ahead of him after football."

"Well, the Stars seemed to make it believable that Aaron killed himself when they brought up his concussions."

"I guess you can't rule that line of thinking out either. There were plenty of signs that pointed to suicide, which is why the police investigation went that way."

"I'm hoping to change that and bring the truth to light."

"Good luck with that. I think they have the truth, but you never know when Charles Robinson is involved."

"Believe me—I already know," Cal said.

They sat in silence as they devoured the rest of their food. Cal thought for a few moments before speaking again.

"Earlier you mentioned that when Aaron was taking PEDs, he didn't seem too concerned with getting caught. Did you find that strange?"

"I've learned that the less I know in the business, the better I sleep at night. So, I didn't exactly find it strange. But I did find the timing of his announcement strange."

"How come?"

"Usually, if there's any league discipline with one of my clients, I get a heads up call several days before it is announced. I have some friends at the league office and they give me a courtesy call. I didn't get one with Aaron."

"So you think the league knew about this for a few days before it was announced?"

"I'm sure they knew ahead of time, probably at least four or five days before."

"And no one called you?"

"Nope. I even called one of my friends there to find out what was going on. He said the first he had seen or heard of it was when it was leaked in the media. It was like they were trying to depict Aaron as some kind of dark and sinister guy, like he was on drugs and wasn't mentally stable getting his head bashed in as a running back. He certainly had his struggles, but it wasn't quite as bad as everyone has claimed. But you just never know about people."

Cal thought for a moment as he scraped his plate with his fork to gather any remnant of barbecue sauce. The picture was clearer but hadn't fully formed yet.

He thanked Franklin for his help and got up to leave. He glanced at the wall as he walked toward the exit and noticed a picture of Charles Robinson and his family smiling with one of the owners.

Cal sneered in disgust. He knew the codger was behind Aaron's death. Now he just needed to know why and how so he could prove it.

CHAPTER 19

CAL SAT ON A BENCH outside of Jackson's in the warm California sun. He needed a few moments of peace. With all that he'd been through, he needed more than just peace. He needed leads. He needed evidence. He needed answers. And none of it was happening quickly enough to suit him.

Once Kelly arrived and picked him up, they debriefed each other on their conversations. Kelly met with several of the nurses who knew Aaron Banks when he volunteered there. But nothing much came of it. They all gushed about how Aaron loved the kids and how generous he was. Based on her brief conversations with the nurses, Kelly determined that his death was a shock, particularly the nature of it. They didn't want to tell the kids, but one of them saw it on TV and started asking questions. The nurses struggled to explain why Aaron would take his own life as had helped them fight for theirs. One nurse said the kids spent the entire day crying once they heard the news.

The nurses were right—it didn't make sense. None of it did. And as Cal dug deeper, he grew more incensed at the way the authorities so quickly dismissed his death as a suicide without any in-depth investigation.

Cal shared with Kelly what he learned from his meeting with Bobby Franklin. It led to more questions than answers, particularly about Aaron's PED usage. Nausea crept over Cal as he thought about having to tell Mrs. Banks that her son was indeed using drugs. She adored her son and that was a truth she would not take too easily.

As the sun began to dip into the Pacific, Kelly veered south onto the 5 and drove toward her apartment. The work ahead of Cal in solving who killed Aaron Banks would be immense—but he kept feeling like there was something else there. Something even bigger, as if Aaron's death was covered up to hide what really happened. He would know more once Kelly's cousin provided him with an autopsy report.

Cal and Kelly said nothing as she drove. He was enveloped in his own sea of speculative thinking, as he suspected Kelly was also. However, it came to an abrupt halt.

Bam!

Cal and Kelly lunged forward as a silver truck smacked into their bumper.

"What the—" Kelly exclaimed before getting rammed again.

"Not again!" she shrieked.

Cal turned around to see the perpetrator—a Dodge Ram with a steel grill on the front. The driver was a young man, perhaps in his late 20s, wearing a baseball cap covered by his hoodie and large reflective sunglasses. He also brandished a pistol.

Cal shouted instructions, urging Kelly to switch lanes. Every time she did, the truck did likewise. After two more bumps and about a minute of heart-pounding driving, Cal urged Kelly to cut off a car on the right and then slow down in an effort to keep the truck from tailing them. She pulled it off like a Hollywood stunt driver. The driver didn't look too concerned, laughing as he sped past Kelly all while waving his gun out the window.

Maybe it was road rage. This was L.A., after all. Or maybe it was another warning. Cal wasn't interested in taking chances. A brick in the window, an exploding car and being bumped in traffic on the 5 added up to trouble.

"Let's get your stuff from the apartment and stay somewhere else tonight," Cal suggested. "I'm going to get a hotel room. Can you stay with a friend? I'd rather split up since I'm sure they are targeting me. I don't want you to get hurt."

Kelly nodded. Her mascara ran as tears streamed down her face. She bit her lip. Cal watched her fear turn to anger.

"Why does this always happen to us?"

"You mean people trying to kill us?"

"Yes, Cal. I just don't understand."

"Deceit does its dirtiest work in the darkness. We're uncovering the truth—and someone doesn't want it to get out. You know this is never easy."

"I know," Kelly said, sniffling. "I always want to expose the truth until we start to do it. I can't take much more of this."

"Don't worry. I feel like we're close. Once we report the truth, no one will hurt us."

"I hope you're right—I hope we stay alive to tell it."

Cal put his hand on Kelly's knee, giving her a reassuring squeeze. He decided to get a room at a hotel nearby one of her friends' apartment, where she would stay. So far, the gate to Kelly's apartment proved meaningless and she was more interested in getting a good night's sleep—and knowing that she was safe when she put her head on her pillow.

She didn't look at Cal as she wiped away more tears while staring at the road.

"Tomorrow, we fight back," he said.

CHAPTER 20

CAL AND KELLY MET at the hotel around ten o'clock on Sunday morning. He wanted Kelly to get into the stadium early, while he thought it best that he wait later before entering the press box. There were people he wanted to talk with before the Stars likely tossed him out—and he needed to make sure they were there.

Cal gave Kelly explicit instructions on who to photograph. He needed certain pictures to gain leverage in order to get the information he needed, none of which would be happening on the field. He texted her a reminder, attaching photos of people she needed to capture on film with Robinson. It was a lengthy list, but Kelly was already scanning Robinson's box with her powerful telephoto lens. She was going to be ready.

To pass the time, Cal sat in the car and listened to the experts talk about the game—and about the city council's impending stadium vote on Tuesday. The result on the field would impact the playoff hopes of both teams. And with the Raiders on the verge of breaking a long playoff drought, the stakes soared. The atmosphere even felt more like a game in January than late November. The result from Tuesday's council meeting would be met with equally exciting fanfare.

Cal stared out the window at fans circled around grills, drinking beer and debating sports. He wondered what people would think if they really knew what went on behind the scenes—the drugs, the power struggles, the sabotage. He had seen it all while covering the NFL in the past. They likely wouldn't care—as long as their team won. It's the same way Americans viewed the government. They shrugged at scandals as long as they had jobs and were left alone to enjoy their own prosperity.

Cal believed truth and justice were virtues worth fighting for. It's why he didn't back down from a bully like Robinson. Fear only gripped him when he thought about what could happen to Kelly. But as long as he could wield a pen, he welcomed the conflict. Most of his peers in the sports writing community sought the easy road. Just report the facts and follow up on the scandals when someone else broke them. So many of them were fans with laptops. Yet, Cal was a different breed. He had a few friends who viewed the profession like he did. Enjoy the easy days but don't shy away from rolling up your sleeves. Cal often wondered how he ended up as a sports writer in the first place. His skill set was more suited for unearthing political scandals than frivolous sports' controversies. But this one felt different. This one felt much more far reaching and sinister.

Of course, Cal had never faced a giant before like Robinson. Based on the events over the past week, Robinson had a firm grasp on every vein that might lead to the truth—and he was squeezing the life right out of them. Cal needed to resuscitate them, even if it was just one. He needed to throw Robinson off and put his attention elsewhere.

Thirty minutes before kickoff, Cal made his way to the press entrance. The lines at the fans' gates appeared surprisingly short for this close to kickoff. But Cal could hear from the stadium buzz that most of the fans were already in the stadium, calling for blood. The Raiders seemed to bring out the worst in opposing fans, particularly other teams in California. Cal enjoyed soaking in the atmosphere, even though he wasn't writing a single word about it today. He noted that if felt more akin to a prison on the brink of a riot than a football game between two rivals.

Once inside the press box, Cal sought out one of his friends. He needed to find a place to publish his story, if it ever came to that point. He looked on the seating chart for a few of his friends. He noticed Marty Price's name on the list. Marty ran RazorSharp.com, one of the best independent sports websites for California sports. Its readership was small in comparison to other national websites, but it was read closely by writers and bloggers for Yahoo!, ESPN and CBS Sports. Once, Marty broke a story about one of the L.A. Clippers players who was involved in a point-shaving scandal. Within 30 minutes of posting the story, ESPN was all over it. If he could convince Marty that the story was true, RazorSharp.com would be a perfect home for such an expose on Charles Robinson and the mysterious death of Aaron Banks.

Cal discreetly found Marty and made his pitch. Marty didn't make any promises but said he would consider it if the story contained proper sourcing and evidence. It wasn't the immediate affirmation Cal hoped for, but it was something.

Robinson's box was close to the press box. Cal noticed a few guests in Robinson's box. It was exactly what he was hoping for. He texted Kelly.

I hope u r taking pix of CR's box

The replay came back quickly.

oh yes

Cal smiled. He had all the ammunition he needed to send Robinson into a panic and put him on the defensive.

He then made his way to his assigned seat on press row, eyeing the carnage of what was once the media buffet. Only a few tin trays filled with dingy liquid and an overcooked steak remained along the buffet line. He shook his head and smiled. If there was one word to describe all sports writers, it was *hungry*.

Cal sat next to Dave Thornton, the Raiders' beat writer for *The Chronicle*. He shot Cal a surprised look.

"What are you doing here?" Dave asked.

"I was in town. I had a pass. What else was I going to do?" Cal asked.

"Well, you better get up. That's not your seat."

"What?" Cal asked, looking at the nametag with his name on it. "That's my name right there."

Cal felt a tap on his shoulder. He turned around to see Hardman.

"Well, if it isn't the unemployed sports writer," Hardman said, smirking. "I believe you're in my seat."

Cal stood up.

"Listen here you little son of a—"

"No, no, no. No profanity allowed in the press box, Mr. Murphy," Hardman interrupted. "You might get away with that while covering rousing chess club tournaments, but we professional writers keep it clean up here."

A few of the writers nearby snickered at Hardman's inane suggestion that press box talk was genteel. Cal scoffed at Hardman's snarky comment.

"You stole my story, you worthless hack," Cal said. "I should've known you might try to leach off of me."

"Please," Hardman said, dismissively. "I was just doing my job, something you should've done a long time ago. Maybe one day you'll understand the meaning of the word *scoop*."

With each exchange, Cal and Hardman's voices grew louder, so loud that it drew the attention of press box security.

Hardman turned toward the approaching guard and told him Cal was in his seat.

Cal tried to protest, but spun around to see Robinson standing in the press box, waving arms wildly at a guard as he pointed in Cal's direction. The guard joined the disturbance and took charge.

"Cal Murphy, come with me," he said. "Your pass has been revoked."

Cal didn't resist, walking peacefully out of the box. He looked back at Hardman, who hadn't yet sat down, apparently enjoying his triumphant ejection of Cal.

Cal then turned to see Robinson. The Stars' owner's face appeared snarled and twisted as he glared at Cal.

"Don't you ever come back here again," Robinson said. Then he learned in closer and said in a whisper, "I can't stress how important it is that you end this little charade you call an investigation now, especially if you ever want to get paid another penny for a word you write."

Cal didn't back down. He calmly whispered back, "I'm gonna nail you to the wall, you bastard."

Robinson immediately started screaming and yelling threats at Cal. Cal just smiled as the guards forcefully led him out of the room and out of the stadium. Mission accomplished.

CHAPTER 21

CAL SAT IN THE CAR and listened to the game on the radio. Playing with heavy hearts, the Stars struggled. Perhaps it had more to do with their quarterback being suspended than their backup running back having died earlier in the week. Either way, it led to a rout for the Raiders. The Raiders led 24-3 at halftime and fans came pouring out of the stadium.

Cal would never consider leaving any game early. It was also his job to stay until the end, but even when it wasn't he remained in his seat until the last out was made or the last second ticked off the clock. He once went to a Mariners-Red Sox game with one of his college buddies, which included the privilege of taking his friend's five-year-old brother. The kid got restless and wanted to leave early. With Jamie Moyer and Curt Schilling locked in a tight pitcher's duel, Cal did everything he could to keep the kid satisfied. But by the time the ninth inning rolled around, Cal had exhausted all his tricks. They were all walking out of the stadium when John Olerud hit a two-run homer in the bottom of the ninth to win the game for Seattle. Cal vowed never to leave early again. It was out of principle. Keep fighting until the end because you never know what break you're going to catch.

Robinson's antics in the press box gave Cal a big break. With so many witnesses and some motivation that was public knowledge, Robinson would have to back off now. And even if he didn't, he would after Cal moved to the next phase of his plan to buy more time.

* * *

At the end of the third quarter, the Raiders held a 27-10 lead. Cal predicted there would be no stirring comeback by the Stars either. Not that he would be allowed in the stadium to watch it even if it did. His work was almost done.

Cal's phone buzzed. It was Kelly.

"I'm leaving now. Where are you?"

"I'm at the car."

"At the car?"

"Yeah, I got kicked out. I'll have to tell you all about it. Did you get the pictures?"

"Oh, yeah. They're perfect."

"Great. Hurry back."

Cal hung up. He and Kelly made a great team. He didn't like dragging her into such complex investigations, often fraught with danger. But she liked it and he enjoyed her company. And she was good at what she did.

Once she got back to the car, they left the stadium. The game was still in the early stages of the fourth quarter, making for a quick exit from the stadium parking lot. During the drive back to Cal's hotel, Cal related what happened in the press box incident. Kelly squealed and clapped her hands a couple of times when Cal redelivered his parting shot to Robinson. Cal felt like doing the same thing when he saw Kelly's pictures.

Upon entering Cal's room, he opened his laptop and they began downloading Kelly's pictures. Her zoom lens produced pictures so clear that it was as if she was standing in the press box with them snapping grip-and-grin photos.

Cal dragged the ones he was interested in to a new folder on his desktop. He continued sifting through the images until he came across one that made him start to think.

"Do you know who these guys are?" Cal asked.

"One of them is Robinson's son, right?

"Son-in-law," Cal corrected. "What about the other guy?

Do you recognize him?"

"No, not really. You just said to keep my camera trained on Robinson's luxury box and his guest box. That was from his guest box. Do you recognize him?"

"Yes. I also think I know why Aaron Banks was murdered."

* * *

The sun was slipping down into the Pacific Ocean when Charles Robinson slumped into his office chair. He had no reason to celebrate, so he punished himself with a glass of less expensive Scotch.

Swilling the amber liquid around in his glass, he pondered his next steps to mitigate the growing disaster that was Cal Murphy. Everything he worked for could come crumbling down, though he felt confident Cal's credibility would come into question after he spread the word that Cal had been plagiarizing. It wasn't true, of course, but it only took a few swift strokes to his archived articles on *The Chronicle*'s website by a hungry intern to fix that. Robinson made sure dead ends would appear when Cal least expected him.

It wasn't a permanent solution, but a temporary one would have to suffice. Today, Robinson had lost his cool and showed his true colors. It was a costly mistake, but one he could fix. He just needed some more time, something he was in short supply of.

CHAPTER 22

WITH THE RISE OF SOCIAL MEDIA, news reporting devolved into a race to be first, facts be damned. Being the first news agency out in front of a story meant bragging rights, often times with scooped reporters forcing themselves to cite a competing news agency's name in their on-air reports or online articles. The entire article wasn't even necessary when it came to social media. A titillating headline sufficed. And if you were wrong? Scrub your social media feed and the problem was solved. The occasional ridicule from the public paled in comparison to sticking it to the competition.

Cal loathed Twitter. His @CalMurphy24 account languished with several hundred followers, most of whom only followed him so they could mock him. If Cal wrote a story about the rise of a good young quarterback, fans took to Twitter to blast him, excerpting partial sentences with the player's dismal stats. It made fans feel superior to an "expert." It had become a sport in its own right—and a vicious one at that.

For all of social media's irritating traits, getting news out fast was the golden nugget Cal embraced today. He put Robinson on his heels by drawing his ire in the press box on Sunday. Today, he was going to send him running. All Cal had to do was find one willing blogger to stoke the fire of a nasty rumor.

As soon as he woke up early on Monday morning, Cal called his friend Trip Cantley. Trip blogged for DeadOn.com, which regularly engaged in click-bating stories. The website amassed millions of hits each day, using the gallery of cheerleaders to hook users. But for those who visited the site for more than just pictures, there were some well-sourced articles written by sharp bloggers. Trip was one of those bloggers.

Cal told Trip what he knew. It wasn't a full-fledged report that he offered, but Cal's pitch was enough to draw Trip's interest. And he knew it would draw readers' interest, too. Cal emailed Trip the photo and a few notes. Such inside information gave Cal the title of "sources close to the organization", enabling Cal to remain anonymous. All he had to do now was sit back and wait for the Internet explosion to take place.

* * *

Miles Kennedy sipped his coffee, piping hot and straight. He chided reporters for adding anything to their daily caffeine shots. "Real reporters drink their coffee black," Kennedy always said, "not this mamby-pamby double-shot soy latte crap." Interns usually took the brunt of his tirades with comments like, "Why put coffee in your drink when all you want is sugar and milk?" Seeing someone dress up their coffee usually made Kennedy grumpier than if he skipped coffee altogether.

Kennedy didn't see anyone committing such a cardinal sin today, but he was still cranky, perhaps more than he had ever been. And it was more than just being another Monday. Despite scooping every paper over the weekend on L.A. Stars' Isaiah Smith's suspension due to drug use, Kennedy burned over having to fire Cal. He recognized Cal's potential as a reporter and resented the fact that he wouldn't be able to nurture him any further. More than that, he cared about Cal and wanted to know how he was doing.

Kennedy dialed Cal's number.

They exchanged awkward pleasantries. Such small talk seemed forced.

"I just want you to know that if I ever get a chance to hire you back, I will," Kennedy said. "That is, if you'd like to work for me."

"Thanks. I appreciate that. I know your hands were tied. And I hate to tell you this, but you're going to have more fun with hands-tied reporting in the coming days."

"What are you talking about?"

"You'll know soon enough," said Cal, remaining cryptic. "That is unless you're willing to part with the company line."

* * *

It was 10 a.m. and Cal grabbed his bag and headed to the airport. He needed to be back in time to attend Aaron Banks' memorial service on Tuesday morning as well as pick up Kelly's cousin, who had agreed to perform another autopsy on the dead NFL star. Kelly had secured three personal days to return with Cal to San Francisco. He certainly didn't mind the company. She didn't mind escaping the city where she had been assaulted twice in less than a week.

Cal met Kelly at the airport for their noon flight to L.A. They had a tight schedule for their time in San Francisco. It wasn't exactly the way he would've wanted to spend time with Kelly, but any time was better than no time. Seeing her every day for over a week straight was a luxury rarely afforded.

Once they got through the security checkpoint, they found their way to the gate. Cal was anxious to discuss their next move in the investigation.

"Did you set the bomb?" Kelly asked as she smiled.

Cal glared at her in disbelief.

"Kelly, this is an airport. Don't joke like that here," he said, looking around to see if anyone heard her.

No one was within earshot. Then he continued.

"I sent everything to Trip. We'll see what he does with it."

Kelly changed subjects quickly.

"The LAPD called me this morning."

"Oh? Did they tell you who blew up your car?"

"They said it was gang related. Apparently, Honda Accords are popular among drug dealers. They told me about some gang related shooting involving a black Honda Accord less than two miles away from my apartment complex. They think it was retribution but they got the wrong car."

"What about the note on the door?"

"They said it wasn't written for me."

"That sounds shady to me, like someone's on the take."

"Does everyone have to be on the take, Cal? I swear you're the most suspicious person I know."

Cal raised his defenses. "And you think I don't have reason to be? There are just too many coincidences to make me think you weren't being targeted. A brick through the window, a blown up car and a road rage incident. You can't tell me those aren't related somehow."

"Maybe they are. But right now, I'm taking some solace in their report. I'd like to think I'm not the target of some secret assassin."

"Don't be so naive."

Kelly furrowed her brow and crossed her arms. She wanted to feel safe. She needed to feel safe. And if the police report made her feel that way, Cal needed to drop it.

"Look, I'm sorry," Cal said, putting his arm around an unreceptive Kelly. "I just don't want you to get hurt, OK?"

She nodded but said nothing, staring blankly out a glass window at a jet roaring off the ground.

Cal got up to get something to eat, offering to bring back Kelly something. She declined, still seething over Cal's comment. It was a lame apology at best.

He walked straight toward "Home Turf Sports Bar", his favorite place to kill some time while waiting for the flight to begin boarding. Before he got there, his phone started buzzing, alerting him to the arrival of several new text messages.

Are you watching this?

And another one:

Did you start this rumor?

Then one from Kennedy:

Thanks a lot!

Cal then hastened his gait. He needed to get in front of a television and find out if everything worked.

The television in the bar was tuned to ESPN. Two talking heads blathered on about the playoff chances of the Raiders after Sunday's big win. But it was the news scrolling across the bottom that drew a discreet fist pump from Cal.

"BREAKING: Sources report Stars owner mulling move to Toronto."

But that wasn't all. It was the next line that caused Cal to smile.

"L.A. City Council postpones vote on stadium deal indefinitely."

CHAPTER 23

CAL SLIPPED OUT EARLY to go to Seaside Cemetery alone. The early morning sun glistened off the bay as a brisk wind whipped through the grounds. Cal was glad he wore his shades and a stocking cap, partially because of the weather but also to serve as a disguise. He didn't want to detract from the memorial service for Aaron Banks. And while he wouldn't be the one causing a commotion, Charles Robinson might if he saw Cal.

Despite the private nature of the service, Cal estimated there were at least 300 chairs set out, most of which were already taken once he arrived. To accommodate the crowd, the service was held in another portion of the grounds, apart from the burial site. Mrs. Banks sat on the front row, decked out in standard black attire, including a lace veil attached to the front of her large black hat. Not a word had been uttered and she was already dabbing her tears, crying softly. Aaron Banks' titanium casket remained closed. Cal knew his body wasn't inside, but it was still a sobering visual. It didn't seem fair to Cal that a few poor choices led to Banks' sudden demise. If that's all it took to end up six feet under, Cal would have been there long ago.

Cal scanned the crowd for Robinson and noticed him almost immediately. Robinson always carried a billionaire's entourage with him. His included a flakey blonde assistant in her 20s—someone too young to have grown tired of the pompous codger—along with a late-30s yes man and two other team officials. It would be easy to avoid him now.

At eleven o'clock, the funeral grounds chapel chimed, marking the beginning of the service. It dragged on with frequent interruptions from Mrs. Banks' wailing along with other young women who just couldn't control their sorrow. Cal wasn't sure who the other women were, but he presumed they were Banks' various love interests at different times in his life. It pained Cal to observe the whole scene.

Finally, the minister spoke. Dr. R. G. Wright took command of the service and seized the attention of everyone in the crowd. As head of one of the Bay Area's largest churches, Dr. Wright was well-respected for his moderate stance on many social issues that he said did nothing but distract the church from its central mission, which was "to show the world God's love." He was also a pastor to San Francisco's stars. Whenever local celebrities were in crisis, it seemed like they always sought out Dr. Wright. He oftentimes became the *de facto* spokesperson for those in the limelight struggling with their success—or their failure. So when he spoke about Aaron Banks, it felt like it was first-hand knowledge rather than a second-hand story.

"Most of us will remember Aaron for his God-given ability to play football," Dr. Wright said. "He brought stadiums to their feet as crowds of adoring fans chanted his name following a touchdown or a fantastic play. It was something he was good at, excelling easily. But he did other things too when no one was looking, like volunteering at the children's cancer ward of St. Mark's Hospital. There was no adulation, no endorsement deals to be had, no forward-thinking career moves. It was just Aaron and his kids.

"I once visited Aaron's house for dinner while traveling to Los Angeles last year. Over the years, I've had the privilege to go inside the homes of many famous celebrities. And one of the things I always want to see is their trophy case. For some people, it might be their Oscar or Grammy. Or for athletes, they like to display championship rings and MVP awards. Aaron won plenty of accolades throughout his career, and I was anxious to see how they were displayed.

"But as I looked around, there weren't any to be found. So, I asked him where they were. And he said in all sincerity, 'Dr. Wright, you know I don't care about that stuff. Let me show you what's really important to me.'

"He led me toward the beginning of a hallway and flipped the light on for me. And what was hanging on the wall? Drawings from kids at the cancer ward lined both walls all the way down the hall. Then he looked at me and said, 'Everything I do now is for these kids—even playing football. Once football is over, this is what I want to do. I want to give kids hope and show them love.'

"This was something Jesus did. Even his disciples weren't thrilled to see a bunch of children interrupting their master's time. But that's when Jesus explained just how important that time is. In the eighteenth chapter of the Gospel of Luke, Jesus told his disciples, 'Let the children come to me, and do not hinder them, for to such belongs the Kingdom of God. Truly, I say to you, whoever does not receive the kingdom of God like a child shall not enter it.'

"Now, Aaron didn't have any biological children of his own. Then again, neither did Jesus. But that doesn't matter. Long after we stop thinking about Aaron's amazing feats on the football field, there will be kids—kids who will be all grown up—that will never stop thinking about how a professional football player paid attention to them when they were at their weakest. They will always realize that they matter.

"And that's how I want us to remember Aaron today. I want us to remember him as someone who believed everyone mattered, even the least of the least. It was something about his character that stood in stark contrast to the me-first attitude of professional athletes today. It's refreshing. And it's a shame that he left this world earlier than he had to."

Cal caught himself whisking away a tear before anyone noticed him. Not that there was anything wrong with crying at a funeral. But Cal was a journalist. He wasn't supposed to get emotionally attached to his subjects. His job was to tell the story, present the facts. The public decided how they wanted to interpret them or respond. Yet, here he was crying over Dr. Wright's moving and inspirational story about Aaron's life.

A few friends shared similar stories about Aaron before the service finally drew to a close. It made Cal resent his journalistic code of objectivity, so much so that he determined to dispose of it almost entirely. He didn't care anymore what stood between him and proving Robinson had Banks murdered. It emboldened Cal, making him forget about his initial instinct to avoid the Stars' owner. Instead of avoiding him, Cal decided to confront him. He needed to stir Robinson up, get him to make another mistake. It was the only way Cal believed he could force the billionaire to show his hand.

Cal waited for the service to conclude before approaching Robinson, who was in no hurry to get to his limousine. A pack of reporters hovered around Robinson's car, awaiting his arrival. He strode slowly down the hill until he heard a voice that arrested his attention.

"It's a shame Aaron Banks had to die so young, isn't it?" Cal said. With both his hands stuffed in his coat pocket, Cal exuded confidence—the confidence of a man with nothing to lose.

Robinson spun in Cal's direction.

"Why you son of a—" Robinson said as he strode toward Cal and away from the media cameras.

Cal walked backward slowly before stoking Robinson's anger again. "It's OK, Charles. I know you're angry. I heard about the city council's decision to postpone the vote on the new stadium. Tough week for you."

Cal wasn't just pushing Robinson's buttons—he was mashing them with a sledge hammer.

Robinson stopped just short of Cal, invading his personal space and leaving him vulnerable and uncomfortable. But Cal held his ground.

"You listen here, you worthless hack," Robinson began. "I know what you're up to, but if you think I'm going to be intimidated by you and your little games, you've underestimated me. I'm going to make it my personal mission to make sure you never get a respectable writing job for the rest of your life."

Cal laughed. "You think slaving away at one of your papers was ever respectable? I'm afraid you overestimate your self-importance. Besides, I don't know any murderers who run what I would call respectable businesses."

"I don't like what you're insinuating. But if you keep it up, I might just dig a hole and bury you in it myself."

"Is that a threat?"

"It's a promise!" Robinson said before storming off to his car.

Cal pulled his phone out of his pocket and turned off the app that recorded his entire conversation. Hopefully it would be enough to convince the last remaining detectives not on Robinson's payroll to look into him if Cal somehow ended up missing. He attached the recording and immediately emailed it to Kelly and Gregory from his phone. Insurance was just as important as proof at this point in Cal's investigation.

Cal lingered to watch the media show with Robinson. He watched Robinson vanish in a sea of cameras and microphones. Cal couldn't hear what Robinson was saying, but his body language conveyed his response: it was a ridiculous rumor and he had no plans of leaving Los Angeles.

And it was a ridiculous rumor, one Cal had helped birth. To give a rumor legs, the appearance of truth needed to be there—and Cal made sure all the ingredients were present. Carl DuBois was a wealthy Toronto businessman who often declared that should the NFL ever want to expand into Canada, he would be an eager owner with the necessary capital to buy in. DuBois also built his wealth on the back of the newspaper industry, though he was more famous for his designer watches. The DuBois time-piece collection served as a status symbol among the wealthy. It grew out of a small investment DuBois made, morphing into an international conglomerate that ran the gamut of accessories, such as purses and wallets. Almost everyone had forgotten about DuBois' ownership—and true passion—the newspaper business.

When Cal interviewed Robinson, he noticed a ticket enve-lope sitting on Robinson's desk with DuBois' name scrawled on the outside. DuBois was there to talk about buying some of Robinson's newspapers in the upstate New York area, not the moving of an NFL team. But newspapers reporting about newspapers always made for dull news. The rumor dripped with truth even after it had been marinated in deceit.

Satisfied with the spectacle, Cal looked back toward the service site. He took a moment to gather his thoughts and com-posure before approaching Mrs. Banks. He wanted to pay his respects again, but he also wanted to make sure she was still will-ing to allow the independent autopsy to continue.

He trudged up the hill toward her and caught her when she was left alone for a minute.

"Mrs. Banks, I wanted to let you know again that I'm sorry for your loss," Cal said.

"Thank you, Cal. I appreciate all your support and help in finding out the truth behind Aaron's death."

"You're welcome. After hearing those stories about him today, I'm more convinced than ever that someone was behind this. And I think it's a far more diabolical plot than I could've ever imagined."

"What do you mean?"

"I mean, I think that Aaron's death wasn't random. I think it was plotted out for several months. But I need that autopsy to help prove this. You're still OK with the independent autopsy being performed, aren't you?"

"Yes, I am. I'm OK with anything that will clear my son's good name and catch his killer."

Cal smiled and nodded before bidding her goodbye. He was going to make sure Mrs. Banks got her wish.

He climbed into his car and turned the radio on. Tuned to 95.7 The Game, Cal listened to the talking heads breaking down the Monday Night Football game. The Dallas Cowboys' star wide receiver had suffered a serious head injury and missed the remainder of the game due to a concussion. The radio personalities began talking again about concussions as if they were scientific experts, which annoyed Cal to no end. Yet he listened intently when the subject shifted slightly.

That's why companies like Head Gear are poised to help save football. Their proprietary helmets are engineered to reduce the risk of concussion by ninety-five percent. And I can tell you I'm super excited I about their initial public offering next Monday. I told you guys this is only the third stock I've done this with—and the other two were for Google and Apple.

The other host began questioning why he was still working as a sports radio personality when he could either be a financial investor or have enough money to retire and be independently wealthy by now.

Cal turned the radio off. The banter disgusted him. He didn't believe profiting on other people's fear and pain was a noble business model.

CHAPTER 24

TED SIMPSON HAD WAITED patiently for Cal to return to San Francisco. There was some unfinished business they needed to clean up. Though Ted was certain Cal dismissed him as a vindictive jerk, he figured Cal would still be eager to meet with him. The likelihood that anyone had put the pieces together about Robinson was low, especially in a media market that begged for L.A.-style scandals. It seemed Hollywood owned those scandals and refused to share. So far, only Cal had stuck his nose where it didn't belong and he was about to lose his head, if not his mind.

Ted dialed Cal's number.

"This is Cal."

"Hi, Cal. This is Ted."

Ted could feel Cal's blood pressure rising over the phone.

"What are you doing calling me? I thought I made it pretty clear that I didn't want to speak to you again."

"Wait, wait, wait. You did, but I wanted to apologize. I can't really get into all the reasons now why I told you those things, but we need to meet and talk in person."

"What things? The lies or that the lies were lies? I can't keep your stories straight, Ted. And I doubt you can either."

Convincing Cal to meet wasn't going to be easy for Ted.

"Look, I understand where you're coming from. Believe me, I really do. But some of these things I just can't go into right now. How soon can you meet?"

Cal reluctantly agreed to meet late Thursday morning with Ted. It wasn't as soon as Ted hoped, but it would have to do.

* * *

Later that afternoon at LAX, Cal watched Kevin Mendoza wrestle with his bag as he walked toward he and Kelly. He and Kevin were acquainted with one another on a previous story Cal worked on. On that case, Kevin needed some persuasion to tell the truth about why dead teenagers were popping up all over small town Idaho. Cal suspected that convincing Kevin to explain the truth of what happened wouldn't be necessary this time.

Kevin meandered methodically toward them. He was a bit on the portly side with thinning brown hair and a pair of thick glasses that required constant repositioning on his nose. But for what he lacked in first impressions when it came to his appearance, he made up for it with his meticulous reports. Cal would have never been able to solve the mystery in Statenville several years ago without Kevin's help.

Kelly gave Kevin a big hug. Since Kelly moved from Idaho, she rarely saw Kevin. Their relationship had been reduced to two visits per year—once at Christmas and once during the summer for the Mendoza family reunion. They weren't close, but they were united by a trait that wasn't very welcome in their family: they were the last two Mendoza cousins who were still single.

Cal shook Kevin's hand as the usual post-flight small talk commenced. It consumed the entire 10-minute walk to Cal's car before the most pressing topic was broached—the reason Kevin was in L.A.

"I'm still not sure why I'm here," Kevin said as he climbed into the backseat of Cal's car.

"You're here because I need an independent review of the

coroner's initial report," Cal answered. "You are going to tell me whether this guy committed suicide or whether he was murdered."

Cal eyed Kevin in his rearview mirror. Kevin stared out the window, apparently lost in thought.

"Why do you think he was murdered?" Kevin asked.

"I have a million different reasons why, none of which I can confidently pursue without you telling me if I'm right or not."

"OK, fair enough. I still don't understand why you couldn't get a local doctor to do this."

"We didn't want to raise suspicion about my investigation. Aaron Banks is a big star around here and if anyone got wind of what we were doing, it wouldn't be good."

Kevin paused and then leaned forward, staring at Kelly.

"What have you dragged me into?" he asked.

"A little excitement, Kevin. Just relax. It will be fine. We'll get you right back to looking at dead potato farmers once you take a look at him."

Kevin slumped back into his seat and folded his arms. Nothing excited him about this trip.

"Just know, I'm only doing this for you, Kelly," he said. Cal wondered if Kevin was still sore over his past coercion tactics. Since then, Cal had changed plenty, though he wasn't sure what he would have done anything different to urge Kevin to comply with his demands.

Cal concluded the conversation by going over his plans for the next day. There was still plenty of work to do in order to link Charles Robinson back to the death of Aaron Banks.

* * *

While Kevin and Kelly caught up in the living room, Cal retired to his room to pore over his notes. So many threads dangled in this case, none of which seemed to make a tight seam to pull it all together.

He stared at the photo on his screen. This had to be the missing link—this had to be the way Robinson controlled so many different enterprises without getting his hands dirty.

Cal pulled out his phone and called *The Chronicle's* lead business reporter, Bud Pritchett.

"Hey, Bud. I was wondering if you could help me out. What do you know about Charles Robinson's son-in-law, Carlton Hightower?"

"Oh, that's a ball of yarn I've been wanting to pull the string on for years," Bud said.

CHAPTER 25

CHARLES ROBINSON ALWAYS ARRIVED early to his office. Though mostly out of a strong desire to avoid L.A.'s morning traffic, he also did it out of habit. His father preached to him the value of a good work ethic and how you could achieve anything you wanted in life if you worked hard enough. Robinson clung to the part about a good work ethic, but he knew the rest of that tripe was a lie. People liked to say that America was the land of opportunity, but he knew firsthand that was far from true. America was the land of the lucky entrepreneurs and the conniving capitalists. Many successful businesses translated some luck into a thriving business model. But they would've never achieved what they did without luck. These business owners may not like to admit it, but it was true. Robinson hated luck. He even loathed seeing some low life blue-collar worker suddenly win the lottery and come into millions of dollars. But conniving capitalist? Robinson turned that into a science.

And it also brought him in even earlier than usual. Cal Murphy had been a one-man wrecking crew to his plans with his nosy journalism. He was a problem that needed to be put down like a rabid dog.

Robinson dialed the numbers into his burner phone and awaited the caller to pick up.

"Hello?" came the voice on the other end.

"What are you doing? I thought I told you to take care of

our little problem."

"I'm going to take care of it tomorrow."

"You sure about that?"

"Yes, I'm sure."

"If you don't, I'm going to have someone else do the job with a little extra side job thrown in—and that side job is going to be done. Do you understand me?"

"I do."

"Good. Now get it done. If I don't hear back from you by tomorrow at eight o'clock, I'm getting someone else to clean up your mess."

He slammed the phone down and loosened his tie. It was far too early in the day to be uptight, but Robinson couldn't help it. The walls of his empire could crumble if he wasn't more diligent to eliminate problems. He had underestimated Cal Murphy's skills—but Robinson still held all the power for now.

* * *

Cal got up early to review his notes from his discussion with Bud the night before regarding Carlton Hightower. Despite his in-depth investigation, Cal still lacked the evidence he needed to go to an editor with his findings. And even if he could find an editor to stick his neck out for him, Cal still lacked the definitive proof that Robinson was behind Aaron Banks' death. Even if he could prove it wasn't suicide, Cal couldn't prove who did it. He needed a strong motive, one that superseded the possibility that Banks might turn the Stars into the NFL. For all Cal knew, the league could've known about the Stars' performance enhancing drug program. And if fighting the well-connected, exceedingly-resourced and all-powerful Charles Robinson presented a daunting challenge, Cal didn't want to think about the possibility that his fight might lead him to square off with the NFL. He could have a mountain of evidence, but he would get squashed if they were colluding with Robinson.

Cal decided to put aside hypotheticals for the moment and review what he knew. And it's what he learned about Hightower that had him up so early, sifting through his shorthand notations from the night before.

Bud explained to Cal that Carlton Hightower was the ultimate yes man for Robinson. Who would ever say *no* to his multibillionaire father-in-law who employed him? And when he let you handle some of his investments, you would do whatever he asked.

Until Hightower married Robinson's socialite daughter, Vienna, he was just a low-level hedge fund manager for a large investment firm. Robinson's feud with Vienna over her choice of a husband was messy and public, but Robinson finally relented. Instead of being ashamed of his new son-in-law, Robinson offered Hightower a job. Star Bright Investments funded Robinson's capitalist ventures and hit it big with three or four projects in the first year. Hightower became a superstar among investment circles as a bidding war ensued to retain his services. However, Robinson would have none of it and locked him into a contract with a billion-dollar buyout. It went beyond absurd, but it landed the pair on the front of *Forbes* magazine with the headline: "Billion-Dollar Son-in-Law?"

Bud went on to say how he found out from a source that Hightower was creating offshore shell corporations to funnel money around, mostly to avoid paying taxes. He even gave Cal the name of four shell accounts he knew were created by Hightower.

Cal looked at the names of the corporations: Vienna Connection, The Giant Daily, C.H. Enterprises and Forever Sustainable. Not much originality when it came to naming his shells, Cal thought.

Bud insisted he regularly searched for those names and never found anything on them other than legal filings. But he said he hadn't looked in over a month.

Cal began typing in the names of the corporations, looking for something, anything, that would give him leverage on Robinson, even if it had nothing to do with his report. Everyone knew Robinson was dirty; he just needed to find the string that would unravel it all.

VIENNA CONNECTION

Nothing of consequence on the first page of hits. A low-budget community newspaper website. A few tourist sites. Cal clicked through eight pages worth of results but found nothing.

THE GIANT DAILY

Website listings for sports coverage of the New York Giants. More newspapers sites. Then on the seventh page, Cal found something that made him leap out of his seat and call for Kelly.

"You're not going to believe this! I found a motive for why Charles Robinson would want to kill Aaron Banks!"

CHAPTER 26

REPORTING HAD A WAY of forcing you into the community, whether you liked it or not. While some people may move to a new town for a job and remain virtually invisible unless they took initiative to meet others, reporting afforded no such lifestyle. You were in the public eye from the moment you received your first assignment. Privacy was non-existent, especially if people knew what you looked like. In a matter of months, a good reporter could be one of the most well-connected people in town. It was times like now that Cal appreciated his connectedness.

Once Cal learned that Mrs. Banks was open to having an independent autopsy performed on Aaron Banks, he called Dr. Gerald Steinberg, a professor at UC San Francisco's prestigious medical school. They met once while Cal was writing a piece on the alarming increase of concussions amoung football players and whether it was the result of larger athletes or more stringent detection technology. Dr. Steinberg helped Cal with the story, sharing his medical expertise.

Cal explained to Dr. Steinberg the nature of his request for a place to perform an autopsy without drawing suspicion. Dr. Steinberg said he would be pleased to assist in the process by setting up a lab to process the body. He even said he would be present and serve as a cover should anyone inquire about what they were doing. With Dr. Steinberg around, suspicion would be kept to a minimum.

Cal arrived at the Parnassus Heights campus with Kelly and Kevin in tow. They met Mrs. Banks in the lobby of one of the research buildings and proceeded to the designated lab to meet Dr. Steinberg.

"You ready for this?" Cal asked Mrs. Banks. "There's still time for you to change your mind if you want to."

"As horrifying as this might be as Aaron's mother, I don't know if I'd ever be able to live with myself if I didn't do my part to help find whoever did this to Aaron," she said.

"I'm not sure this will help us find who, but it will certainly tell us if someone else was involved. And I think that's what we're hoping to find."

Dr. Steinberg met the foursome outside the lab door and welcomed them before ushering them inside. The funeral home had transported Aaron's body the day before and it was safe and secured.

Kevin scrubbed up while everyone else made small talk.

"I'll be back to check on you later," Dr. Steinberg said. "Take your time and come find me if you have any questions."

Once Dr. Steinberg left the room, Kevin announced it was time to begin. When he pulled the sheet off the body, Mrs. Banks nearly fainted. She had been through so much already. It wasn't fair that she had to endure watching her son's dead body examined—something a more ethical medical examiner should have already done. Kelly led her to a chair against the wall and gave her a glass of water.

Cal watched intently as Kevin worked his way up and down Aaron Banks' muscular body. It jarred Cal to see such an incredible physical specimen lying dead, his life taken from him in his prime. After spending just 30 seconds admiring his physique in the bathroom mirror each morning, Cal could only imagine the kind of rigorous training necessary to get his body into world class physical shape. An hour every day in the gym—well, if he was honest with himself, a couple of days a week—only kept

Cal from developing an enormous beer gut and wheezing when he walked up more than two flights of stairs. But Aaron Banks could have been a model for a Greek Olympic statue.

Kevin took copious notes, mumbling his findings into a digital voice recorder. Kevin's precise movements and incisions let Cal know that the autopsy was in good hands.

He approached Mrs. Banks, who was still nursing the glass of water Kelly had given her.

Cal asked Mrs. Banks if she wanted to take a walk. She nodded her head in affirmation.

Kelly said she would stay with Kevin and run any interference if necessary while the autopsy was in progress.

"How are you holding up?" Cal asked Mrs. Banks as they stepped into the open air courtyard.

"As best as could be expected under the circumstances," Mrs. Banks said.

She paused.

"You know, the thing that gets me is the fact that Aaron really was using drugs. I can't believe he would voluntarily do that."

"Well, from what I gather, it wasn't so voluntary," Cal answered.

Mrs. Banks stopped. She grabbed Cal's wrist and looked forlorn. "What do you mean?" she asked.

"I mean, I don't think he felt like he had a choice."

Cal started walking again, coaxing Mrs. Banks to join him.

"Oh, come on. That's ridiculous. Aaron had a choice. He didn't have to take any of those drugs. He was a great football player for years without them."

"I know he was. But when I say he had no choice, I mean he was coerced into doing it."

Cal paused before continuing.

"Look, I'm no pro athlete, but I couldn't imagine playing at the highest level in front of thousands of adoring fans every week and suddenly realizing my dream was screeching to a halt.

Not because I wasn't any good any more, but because I wasn't good enough."

Mrs. Banks stopped and stamped her foot.

"I don't buy that either. He was plenty good enough to keep playing. Even if he wasn't in his prime, he was still good enough to start for some other teams. I bet the Bills or the Chiefs would have him any day."

Cal chuckled at Mrs. Banks' dig. Her knowledge of the league also impressed him.

"I'm not saying he wasn't good enough to keep playing in the league. I'm saying he wasn't good enough to keep playing for the Stars—not on his own, anyway. His stats indicated that he was leaving the prime of his career until this year. He wasn't as good as he was several years ago, but he was much improved. And that's unusual for a player his age."

Mrs. Banks sighed and stared at the blue sky.

"I just can't believe I had to bury my baby," she said, tearing up.

Cal rocked back and forth on his feet, unsure of anything he had to say that would comfort the grieving mother before him.

"Well, I think he did it for the kids," Cal finally said. "I think he loved those kids at the cancer center and was willing to sabotage his career just to spend time with them. Maybe he thought he wouldn't be able to once his career was over. But everyone I've spoken to about what kind of man Aaron was talked about his love for those kids."

Mrs. Banks tried to hold back her tears. She looked at Cal and forced a smile. Then she grabbed his left hand and enclosed it in both her hands.

"Cal, you're a good man. I hope you get to the bottom of this and find out who was behind it all. And whoever it is needs to pay for what they did to my son."

Mrs. Banks lingered for a few more moments, clutching

Cal's hands. She finally released it and they both returned to the lab.

When they entered the lab, Cal noticed Kevin furiously scribbling down notes onto a clipboard.

"So, what do you know?" Cal asked.

Kevin stopped and looked up.

"I still have some more work to do, but I can tell you one thing definitely: Aaron Banks was killed by a gun. But he didn't pull the trigger himself – not when the bullet came from at least 75 yards away."

CHAPTER 27

TED SIMPSON ENTERED the secret research facility and flashed his access badge. Located on the Farrallon Islands about 30 miles off the coast of San Francisco, the facility wasn't easy to get to. Supposedly only wildlife researchers lived there—at least that's what the public was told. But there was another research lab there as well. From what Ted observed, some of the research looked legit, while other research looked unethical at best. At least twice he had seen a patient go berzerk in the main lobby only to be restrained with a straight jacket. If he had his druthers, Ted would never set foot on the island again. But he had a reason, a big reason. He had to see his brother.

Nearly ever Wednesday morning, Ted took an hour-and-a-half ferry ride all to spend thirty minutes with his brother. He was instructed to tell his co-workers at PacLabs that he made a supply run on Wednesday mornings to avoid the appearance of favoritism. In actuality, it was the only benefit that kept Ted working there, if you could call it a benefit. It was more like blackmail. Stop working for PacLabs and they would stop paying for his brother's special experimental treatment at the research facility. Ted knew without the treatment, his brother would be dead in a matter of days.

Located on the western side of the island, the facility sat well below the surface. Only a small cylinder block building was visible, looking more like a research station of some sort. It led to an elevator that went down to the actual facility. Despite their best efforts to give the appearance of sunlight, the unnatural light glowing along the walls and faux windows couldn't belie the truth. The sterile hospital aroma slammed Ted's olfactory senses as he walked into the lobby, overriding the appetizing smell wafting from the paper bag in his hand.

Ted smiled at a few familiar faces of staff members as he made his way to Tommy's room. Once Ted darkened the doorway to his brother's room, Tommy perked up, pushing himself up in the bed.

"What did you bring me?" Tommy asked.

"Your favorite, bro."

"A Phat Philly's cheesesteak?"

Ted handed his brother the bag and watched him rip it open and begin to devour the sandwich.

"You're the best."

Ted nodded and smiled.

"So how are you this week?" Ted asked.

"Better. I can tell the latest tweak to my meds has been working," Tommy mumbled with his mouth full of a large bite from his sandwich.

"Well, that's encouraging."

"Yeah, my nurse said if I continue to respond this well, they might be able to release me soon."

"How soon?" Ted asked.

"Another two or three months. I don't know what I'd do with myself. It's really hard to imagine re-entering the real world."

"It's certainly better than this world."

"True. And I wouldn't have to wait for you to bring me my favorite sandwich," Tommy said, pointing to his sandwich with his free hand. "I could get it any time I wanted."

Ted smiled and finally sat down. They talked for a few minutes about the most recent Forty-Niners game and the Giants' new free agent acquisitions. Nothing important.

With only five minutes remaining during his visitation, Ted finally broached the subject he wanted to talk about all along.

"Look, Tommy. I need to tell you something."

"Sure, bro. What is it?"

"Do you know why you're here, getting this special treatment?"

"Yeah, because I have the most awesome brother in the world who is a genius and made a ton of money."

Ted smiled. "Well, only part of that is true."

"Which part?"

"I haven't really made a ton of money."

"What? So, how are you affording all this?"

"I'm not. My employers are paying for it."

"But why?"

"I can't really get into all that, but just know that I'm going to take care of you no matter what."

"What are you trying to say, Ted?"

"I'm trying to say that you're probably going to hear some bad stuff about me in the news in the next couple of days. Just don't believe it. I work for some powerful people and they don't like what I'm doing—and they're going to smear my name. Just think the best about me, OK?"

"What are you talking about?"

"I can't really say right now, but you'll know in due time."

Tommy furrowed his brother and stared at Ted.

"I don't understand."

"You don't have to understand. But I need you to do something for me."

"Anything. You name it."

"Every Friday at 10 a.m., I want you to call this number. If the person there doesn't hear from you, they have instructions to do something, something my employer won't like."

"I'm not sure I like the sound of this."

"It's insurance, Tommy. It's how I'm going to keep you alive."

"Why do you need insurance to keep me alive. What's going on?" Tommy said, growing more confused with each new piece of information out of Ted's mouth.

Ted exhaled a big breath and got up out of his chair. He rubbed Tommy's head before bending over the bed and giving him a big hug.

"I love you, bro." After trading a few slaps on the back, Ted continued. "Just think the best about me. Promise me that. And know I love you, no matter what happens."

"OK," Tommy said. "What's going to happen?"

"You'll see."

With that Ted spun toward the doorway and left the room, pulling the door shut behind him.

Ted hated lying to his brother. He especially hated the fact that a lie was likely the last thing he would ever say to him.

CHAPTER 28

FOLLOWING KEVIN'S PRELIMINARY AUTOPSY findings, Cal grew more determined to bring Charles Robinson to justice for the murder of Aaron Banks. Not that he knew definitively that the Stars' owner was behind it all, but he started to connect the dots, dots that were only circumstantial at this point but impossible to ignore. If for no other reason, he needed to catch Banks' killer for the peace of Mrs. Banks. He had dragged her into this messy investigation out of necessity. But her son was still dead and even more questions arose.

Were he still working for *The Chronicle*—and Charles Robinson wasn't the owner—Cal would be running daily stories on his findings. But those two wrenches necessitated more digging. Cal took solace in the fact that had this all occurred 20 years ago, Robinson would escape unscathed with the public never to hear about his underhanded and illegal dealings. But this was the 21st Century where the gatekeepers for information and news had all but vanished with the boom of the Internet. Robinson couldn't hide forever behind his abusive power. The ship was springing leaks and Cal just needed to find a way to make them all gush forth with the truth. More than anything, he needed a break. He needed to get lucky.

He wondered if maybe he missed something at the bowling alley. Maybe what Ted Simpson was trying to tell him was there all along. Cal told Kelly he wanted to follow up on a few more leads and that he would meet her back at his apartment. He climbed into his car and headed back toward the bowling alley.

On his way to the bowling alley, Cal's phone buzzed. It was Mike Gregory.

"To what do I owe this honor?" Cal answered.

Gregory chuckled. "I hate Hardman?"

"Sounds good to me. What's going on?"

"Well, you know I'm tired of that bastard stealing all your tips and your stories, so I decided to start checking your phone messages one day after I caught him at your desk on your phone."

"How'd he even get my password?"

"You know, Barb, in IT has always had a thing for Hardman. I'd bet she gave it to him."

Cal sighed. "I hate that jerk—so what'd ya find?"

"Well, there was a message from a Detecive Brock from the LAPD who said he has some things he wants to tell you. He said he didn't want to leave it as a message in case someone else listened to it."

"Oh, the irony."

"Yeah, funny, huh? Anyway, he left his cell number and said to call him after three o'clock today when he gets off his shift."

"Perfect, Gregory. I owe you," Cal said.

Gregory relayed the numbers to Cal and hung up.

It was 2:30 and Cal would have to be patient. But he needed to beat Hardman to the call.

CHAPTER 29

CHARLES ROBINSON BELIEVED IN two things in life: himself and contingency plans. He had been in business long enough to know that things never go like you want them to. Very early in his career, Robinson discovered this truth firsthand. No pain felt quite as sharp as a proverbial knife in the back.

Before Robinson ever made his first million—or even hundred thousand—he worked with a group of venture capitalists. They hired him to work as their point person on a major business acquisition. The group already owned a company that dominated the market for X-Ray machines. In an effort to diversify their holdings, the group wanted to purchase a medical digital imaging company that was on the forefront of the changing market and needs within the medical community.

Robinson contacted his mentor to get help on structuring a deal that would be palatable to all involved. Robinson followed his advice and appeared set to deliver a winning deal. But at the last minute, the digital imaging company pulled the deal off the table and was quickly sold to another company. Robinson's mentor had engineered a last-hour coup and left Robinson with nothing but egg on his face.

Such a feeling turned Robinson from a generous and idealistic entrepreneur into a ruthless businessman. If a knife was going to go into someone's back, he was going to be the one jamming it into theirs, not pulling it out of his own. Though he never handled the dirty work, Robinson knew that his contingency plan this time demanded it. He had worked far too long and hard to reach this point in his career to have his beautifully executed plan fall apart on the eve of its launch. Once everything had been set in motion, not even Cal Murphy could stop him.

But everything hadn't been set into motion—not yet, anyway. Cal needed to be eliminated. And if Robinson's man didn't deliver, he would do it himself.

Robinson called his assistant.

"Call Captain Stanfield and tell him to get the plane ready. We've got some business to take care of."

CHAPTER 30

CAL PULLED INTO THE Fun Time bowling alley and parked. He checked his watch. 3:15. He didn't have to wait any longer. *Detective Brock has something to say. No need in making him wait and giving him time to change his mind.*

Cal punched in the numbers on his cell phone and waited. After the third ring, someone answered.

"Detective Brock?" Cal asked.

"Yes. Who is this?"

"This is Cal Murphy from *The Chronicle*. You called and left me a message regarding the death of Aaron Banks."

Cal felt a twinge of guilt for lying. If Detective Brock called back to the paper and asked for him by name with a receptionist, he might learn Cal no longer worked there. For now his secret was guarded by a voice mail message that hadn't been changed by the IT department. However, Cal didn't mind bending the truth if it meant catching a ruthless lawbreaker.

"Oh, right. Thanks for giving me a call back."

Cal listened patiently as Brock described his involvement in the case. He was scheduled to be the lead detective in the next homicide but was asked to let another detective—a Detective Mathis—run point on the investigation. At first, Brock said he didn't think much about the bump. Then he remembered seeing Charles Robinson meeting with the precinct captain and Mathis.

Where it really got interesting was when Brock walked by

Mathis' desk and saw a folder containing the initial police report on Banks' death. Being curious about the high profile death, Brock admitted to snooping around. What he found inside along with the initial report was another report half-filled out with some of the details changed. The first report suggested it was a homicide, while the new report claimed suicide.

"Of course, we all know which report became the official one," Brock concluded.

There was only one thing that mattered to Cal.

"Do you have proof?"

"Yeah, I took a picture on my cell phone of the two reports side by side," Brock said. "While I know most of these guys would jump in front of a bullet for each other, you can never be sure which one might turn around and shoot you themselves—figuratively speaking."

Cal asked Brock to text him the picture and thanked him for reaching out, all with the stipulation that Brock would be an anonymous source in the L.A. Police Department. Before saying goodbye, Cal warned him that another fired reporter named Hardman may give him a call. He said he was posing as a reporter for *The Chronicle* and would ask for this same sensitive information. Cal told Brock not to trust him and suggested he throw him off with another story. Brock agreed and hung up.

A broader picture was beginning to take shape, one that painted Robinson as a grand puppeteer pulling the strings to cover up Aaron Banks' death. He had motive and he had the means to do it. But Cal still needed another piece of evidence or two and had a few remaining questions before taking the plunge and calling the NFL owner and billion-dollar media mogul a murderer. He also wanted to know just how cold-hearted Robinson was, something he wasn't quite sure how to measure.

Cal called Kelly to give her an update on what he had learned. Her exuberance translated well over the phone. Cal pictured her squealing with delight. Both of them were excited about nailing Robinson.

Cal looked at the clock on his dashboard. It was 3:45 p.m.

Just then he noticed three men walking together into Fun Time. All of them wore dark-colored jackets with hoods as well as dark sunglasses.

Maybe 345 isn't a locker number but a time!

Cal waited until the men disappeared inside before springing open his car door and discreetly following them inside. Cal watched as the men grabbed a table in the back corner of the restaurant area, uninterested in bowling. One of the men made eye contact with Cal and got up quickly from the table. He began walking straight toward Cal.

Trying to remain calm, Cal turned toward the main counter and began to ask for a lane and a pair of shoes. Nervously fumbling for his wallet, Cal grabbed it and pulled out a twenty-dollar bill. Cal cut his eyes toward the man again, who was no longer walking toward him but instead walking back to the table with a pitcher of beer. The other two men had already shuffled and dealt a full hand of cards. They didn't look like the sinister group Cal first believed they were.

Three forty-five! What could that mean?

Cal continued his charade, selecting a size 16 bowling ball and typing some initials into the computer adjacent to his lane. Before he put his shoes on, Cal realized he needed to use the restroom.

He pushed the door open with his shoulder to avoid touching it. In a place like this, Cal could only guess when the last time the bathroom was thoroughly cleaned. A few days ago at best. Once the door swung shut behind him, he looked on the chart in a plastic sheath attached to the back of the door. It was blank.

Feeling the urge to go even more strongly, he walked directly to the nearest stall, all the while wracking his brain over what he might have missed. He certainly wasn't interested in bowling by himself at the moment and would rather be uncovering a key piece of evidence.

I've already gotten lucky once today with that phone call from L.A. There's no way I'm getting lucky twice.

Then he remembered what the land lady said to him before the key was stolen, "Don't stall or you might miss it." As Cal began pondering if this was some cryptic message, he saw the numbers "345" scrawled into the tile with an arrow pointing to the left toward the only stall.

Maybe I will get lucky twice.

Cal zipped up his pants and scurried to the stall. It was empty. He locked the door behind him and began looking for anything that might lead him to what Ted was trying to give him. That's when he saw the numbers again, scratched just to the right of the toilet paper holder.

Well, I never thought I'd get lucky in a bathroom stall.

Cal reached underneath the holder and found a thumb drive taped to the bottom. If Ted went to such great lengths to disguise the whereabouts of this drive, Cal figured it must have something important on it. He shoved it into his pocket and raced out of the bathroom. He dropped his shoes off at the desk and continued straight to his car where he fired up his laptop.

He called Kelly as he waited for the computer to boot up.

"I found it!" Cal said as soon as Kelly answered.

"Found what?"

"I found the thumb drive that Ted was trying to hide."

"What's on it?"

"Give me a second. I'm trying to wake my computer up and see."

Cal killed the idle time by sharing with her his sleuthing methods before she made a crack about him being more lucky than good.

Finally, the computer whirred to full power and Cal jammed

the thumb drive into the USB slot. He clicked on a folder. The
he gaped in disbelief.

"Oh my—"

"What is it?" Kelly asked.

"You're not going to believe this. This story just got even
better."

CHAPTER 31

LATE WEDNESDAY EVENING, Robinson's Dassault Falcon 900LX touched down at Half Moon Bay Airport, some 30 miles south of downtown San Francisco. It was a tight runway for takeoff, but he preferred pushing the limits there as opposed to being spotted at a commercial airport. He enjoyed his privacy and wanted the utmost anonymity for this special trip.

He walked out of the plane into a cool ocean breeze blowing across the airfield. Still dressed in his navy power suit, Robinson saw no need to wear anything else. He was still a powerful man and he wasn't about to show any sign of weakness—even if his empire was teetering on the brink of collapse.

Robinson dialed a number on his cell phone and waited for an answer.

"Yeah," said the man when he picked up.

"How are things coming along?"

"Fine. Everything should be completed by tomorrow."

"If I don't hear from you, I'm going to finish the job myself. And I promise you won't like the consequences."

Robinson didn't wait for a response. He hung up and climbed into the black Lincoln Town Car waiting for him.

* * *

Cal and Kelly pored over the files on Ted's thumb drive. Page after page of failed drug tests by some of the league's biggest stars served as titillating information. The real truth was less obvious to anyone who hadn't been digging like Cal had. What was more interesting were the legal papers of incorporation, images of stocks purchased by some of Hightower's shell companies, and Ted's financial documents to his offshore account.

The startup Ted founded with his friends was purchased by PacLabs for a healthy sum, so it was no shock to Cal that Ted even had a large offshore bank account. However, what was shocking were four random large sums deposited into it—all from the same account, presumably Robinson's.

Cal tried to make sense of the dates over the last three years. Random days. Nothing he could make any sense of.

He looked up the first date nearly four years ago to the day—June 25, 2009. Almost immediately, his search engine results were flooded by stories of Michael Jackson's death. Cal decided to search the *L.A. Times* for news on that date and found the murder of a prominent police captain who was shot in an apparent car jacking.

As Cal began searching, he found two more suspicious murders tied to the dates on Ted's ledger. One was of a well-known Los Angeles city councilman, who Cal learned through further research stood in the way of a proposed development by one of the shell companies Hightower managed. To find the other, Ted searched in the Bay area to learn of a former PacLabs employee who was murdered during a home invasion.

"So, what do you make of all this?" Kelly asked.

"I'm beginning to get suspicious of my meeting tomorrow with Ted," Cal answered.

"In what way?"

"I think he's a killer—and I might be his next target."

"That's quite a leap."

"Why? All this evidence points to him being linked to all these suspicious deaths, deaths that were all related to people opposing Robinson."

"You don't know that about the police officer," Kelly protested.

Cal shook his head and thought for a moment.

"Look, that's the only one that might be tough to prove, but if what Detective Brock told me is true then Robinson's tentacles reach deep inside the LAPD. Maybe this officer didn't play nice with Robinson."

"So, maybe that's true, but why would Ted want to kill you? It seemed like he reached out to you to get someone to blow the whistle on Robinson. You weren't even investigating Robinson or anything related to him at the time."

"True. But I've just got this suspicion about our meeting tomorrow."

"Well, we better come up with a backup plan."

Cal and Kelly spent the rest of the evening making phone calls and setting every precaution in place. Walking into the trap of a killer wasn't in Cal's plans for this investigation.

CHAPTER 32

THE NEXT MORNING, Kelly got up early and ventured out for some investigating of her own. She left Cal examining his notes and making a few phone calls to set his a contingency plan in place. After a restless night of sleep, Cal announced that he didn't have any more peace about his impending meeting with Ted Simpson. But Kelly knew Cal—and his courage in the face of danger was admirable yet often borderline insane. She knew Cal wouldn't wait for the storm to come to him. He did what he always did, arming himself the best way a reporter could and running toward the maelstrom, prepared for all its fury. Kelly thought such an approach could get even the best journalist killed, but resigned that so far it hadn't for Cal. All it got him were a truck load of writing awards and national respect and recognition. It wasn't the life Kelly preferred. However, she still liked to dig into stories, especially with Cal. Research specialist was a title better suited for her tastes.

Her assignment was a simple one: track down a man named Brian Bearden and ask him a few questions. Bearden's name surfaced in a list of contacts found on Ted Simpson's thumb drive. Cal easily connected most of the names on the contact list as some type of business associated with Robinson. Contractors, police department employees, media members, PacLabs employees. They all made sense. All of them except Brian Bearden. His name was next to an odd non-profit that neither of them had heard of or could find much information on.

Through some preliminary research, Kelly discovered what seemed like a normal American man. At 37 years old, Bearden lived in a quiet suburban neighborhood with his wife and two children. He worked as a driver for a package delivery service and had no criminal record to speak of. However, Kelly uncovered Bearden's true passion by scouring through his social media pages—coaching youth football. This odd link prompted Cal to ask her to interview him and find out if there was anything there. Besides, she needed something to do while Cal went to meet Ted.

Kelly arrived at the transit station early enough to catch Bearden before he left for the day to begin his late morning route. He was jamming packages into the shelving unit in his van when Kelly approached him.

"Are you Brian Bearden?" Kelly asked.

"Who wants to know?" he asked.

Bearden finished stuffing a package into the van before stopping to look Kelly up and down. Dressed in a khaki uniform with short sleeves and slacks, Bearden's biceps bulged beneath the tight-fitting shirt. His jaw squared and his face covered in stubble, Bearden appeared ready to give out an order at a moment's notice. After being in his presence for ten seconds, Kelly wondered if she might be able to find another way to pass the time.

"I'm, Kelly Mendoza with the Associated Press, and I wanted to ask you a few questions."

"About what?" he said, tensing up for a fight.

"Youth football."

Bearden relaxed. "Oh, well why didn't you say so? That's my favorite thing to talk about. Our team has won the league title two years in a row now."

"You must be proud."

"Oh, I am. But I didn't have anything to do with it. It's those kids who do the hard work and go out and win the championships."

Kelly smiled at his humble-brag before continuing.

"So, Mr. Bearden, I wanted to ask you about your team's affiliation with Equipment for Everyone."

All Kelly could dig up on Equipment for Everyone were a few non-profit document filings and an informational website. Equipment for Everyone served youth sports leagues by helping provide helmets and other equipment for families in need of financial assistance. Based off the information provided on the site, leagues all over the country were signing up to join their program in an effort to enroll more kids in their leagues. Kelly had called the office but received no response. Oddly enough, there wasn't even an answering machine to leave a message. She needed more than that—and a link to Robinson.

"What's this about?" Bearden said, retaking his defensive posture.

"I'm just interested in coaches who participated in the program and what your response was."

"Oh. Well, it was OK, I guess."

"Did you have some kids on your team who used the equipment?"

"Yeah," he said. He paused and then continued. "Look, I know where you're going with this, OK? I invited a few of the dock workers' kids to play. And maybe it was recruiting in a way, but I really wanted to help the kids play football. Their parents couldn't afford to outfit them to play football without some help, so I contacted Equipment for Everyone to see if they could provide a few sets of helmets and pads."

Bearden had no idea where Kelly was going with her line of questioning other than to glean more information about Equipment for Everyone. But she sensed where Bearden was headed and played along.

"So, were these dock workers' kids the best on the team?"

"Well," Bearden began before pausing. "I don't know if I'd say they were the *best*, but they were really good."

As Bearden was speaking, a large man covered in tattoos walked up behind Bearden. The man, presumably a dock worker, sported a crew cut and a reddish tinge on his neck.

"Are you saying Bronco wasn't the best kid out there?" the man interrupted.

Bearden spun around.

"No, no, no. Tank, I wasn't saying that. We all know Bronco was the best linebacker in the league."

The man gave Bearden a firm pat on the arm. "That's more like it," he said before walking off.

Momentarily rattled, Bearden gathered his composure and continued.

"Look, it wasn't recruiting. It was merely providing an opportunity for these kids to play."

"An opportunity made possible by Equipment for Everyone?"

"Yes, they made it happen."

"And what was your experience with them? Was it a good one?"

"Are you here asking about the lawsuit because I thought that was all settled and everything?"

"Maybe," Kelly said, allowing Bearden to believe whatever he wanted for the time being. "Did you hear what happened?"

"Yeah, everything was settled out of court and it was all supposed to just go away."

"It's not always that easy," Kelly said, hoping to coax some more information from Bearden's loose lips.

"That's what they told me," Bearden said, looking at the ground and kicking at rocks that weren't there. "I don't think their helmet had anything to do with the Matthews kid getting a concussion. It's football. Things like that happen. But whenever a big company like Head Gear is involved, they get all nervous and want to make sure there's no bad publicity."

"I'm sorry, did you mean Equipment for Everyone?" Kelly asked.

"No, Head Gear. The company that actually provided the helmets to Equipment for Everyone."

"Did you provide them with some testimonial?"

"Yeah, I did. I mean, I didn't feel the need to mention that one of our kids got hurt wearing their helmet. It's football. It happens. I doubt it had anything to do with their helmet. They had some doctor examine him before he started wearing it and again afterward. He said the injury had nothing to do with the helmet."

Kelly's journalist senses grew keener with each of Bearden's responses.

"Was that before or after they paid you to keep your mouth shut about it?" she asked, trolling a line and hoping for a bite.

"What do you mean? Nobody was supposed to know about that!"

Kelly fished out a picture of Ted Simpson from her pocket and shoved it toward Bearden.

"Was this the guy who paid you?" Kelly asked.

Bearden's beady eyes darted back and forth across the picture, reticent to answer her question.

"I think I know the answer to that question. Thank you for your time, Mr. Bearden," Kelly said as she spun around to leave.

"What did you say your name was again, m'am?" Bearden shouted.

Kelly didn't turn around. She needed to call Cal. The full picture started to come into focus.

CHAPTER 33

TED SIMPSON SCRIBBLED DOWN a letter and sealed it in an envelope. He hated himself for what he had to do. But he'd hate himself even more if he had the power to keep his brother alive and didn't. No matter what Ted did, he felt damned. His impending appointment with Cal Murphy was no different.

Initially contacting Cal may have been one of the stupidest things he ever did. Ted never intended to drag anyone else into his twisted web of a so-called life, but he had. At first, it was under noble pretenses: Ted wanted out. He wanted out of being Charles Robinson's henchman. No longer did he want to live under Robinson's foreboding shadow. No matter how many times he agreed to "just one more job" for Robinson, there were always more. And there was no way out. Not when you were under Robinson's auspices. Not when your brother's life depended on it. Not when a short email to a few media outlets or a police station could ruin you forever.

But that's what it was like when you worked for the most powerful man in California, maybe the entire west coast. Charles Robinson created his fantasy and everyone lived in it, playing their prescribed part. Ted wished he could yank the curtain back on this Oz and expose him. Even then, exposure meant a free press and a free-willed police department—luxuries that didn't exist.

Ted's exit strategy consisted of his best efforts to unveil the truth and protect his brother, something he wasn't sure he could pull off. But he would try. He reeked of desperation.

Sitting in the dusty warehouse off Third Street, Ted listened to the whirring of the dock cranes and the slight lapping of Islais Creek against the few remaining banks a block away. The noise of the shipping industry cluttered the air, making it the perfect location to finish his assignment. The smell of saltwater drifted through the numerous cracks in the wall, also permitting beaming rays of sunshine to light up the floor.

He forced a handful of bullets into his .22 revolver. Any henchman worth his weight in gun powder wouldn't fool with a messy gun that left behind evidence. Who needs to leave empty shell casings lying around, even if you did have the police in your pocket?

Ted jammed the chamber into place and waited for Cal to arrive.

* * *

The vacant warehouse on the corner of Third and Marin Street didn't have a car in the parking lot. That observation caused Cal to grow more angst about his 11 a.m. meeting with Ted Simpson.

Perhaps Ted was running late. That was the more plausible excuse, though city traffic had all but disappeared at this time of day. Or maybe he walked. Or rode his bike. No matter what the reason, it was enough to make Cal jumpy. You don't write award-winning stories by being the most trusting person in the world. Something felt off to Cal, though he wasn't sure what. He wanted to trust his instincts and run. But common sense made way for journalistic instinct—the key to Cal's story rested with Ted.

He texted a short message.

SHOW TIME

Cal slid his cell phone into his pocket and got out of his car.

CHAPTER 34

CAL TOOK A DEEP BREATH and turned the knob, hoping the door would open. It did. This wasn't the first time Cal opened a door with a vast unknown waiting for him behind it. His stomach knotted up as he stepped inside and called out.

"Ted! Are you here? It's Cal?"

No response.

The room appeared to serve as a receptionist area at one time. The only light in the room came from underneath the door and a pair of skylights some 20 feet above on the ceiling. An old aluminum desk with a faux wood top sat in the corner, cleared save an unplugged business phone. A few chairs strewn in front along with a glass coffee table covered in dust made the area look like it might have been a waiting area for clients. The cement floor covered in dirt, sand and grime scritched and scratched beneath Cal's feet as he cautiously walked farther into the room.

"Ted! I'm coming in!"

Cal stopped and listened, hearing a slight scuffling noise along with the intermittent street traffic. Someone was approaching.

"Ted? Is that you?" Cal called out once more.

A shadowy figure appeared in the doorway to the left of the desk. It was Ted.

"Nice of you to make it today," Ted said.

"Thanks for meeting with me," Cal said, refusing to let his guard down.

Cal stared at the revolver tucked into the side of Ted's pants.

"Is that necessary?" Cal asked, gesturing toward the gun.

"Oh, this? Not most of the time, but it is today."

"How come?"

"Now, Cal. Let's not get ahead of ourselves."

"Well, if you're not going to be forthright with me, I'm going to leave right now."

"That's not a good idea," Ted said, pulling out his revolver and pointing it at Cal. "Why don't you have a seat?"

Cal slunk into one of the chairs in the designated waiting area and watched Ted draw closer toward him, gun raised.

"You can put that down now," Cal said.

"No, I can't," Ted said. "You see, I need to make sure you stay for the entire presentation and you hear me out. I have something that needs to be said before we get down to business. And you need to listen very intently. Understand?"

"Sure. Just know I'm not here to hurt you."

Ted aimed the gun at Cal as he walked over to the desk and grabbed a pen and pad sitting on the chair behind the receptionist's desk. He threw them at Cal.

"Here. Take notes with this."

Cal stared at Ted, confused.

What is this guy doing?

Ted paced around the room for several moments before he spoke, constantly cutting his eyes toward Cal. Unsure if this was some sort of test, Cal decided to proceed with caution, jotting down a few questions as he waited for Ted to begin speaking.

"Why am I here, Ted? You're the one who invited me. I don't want any trouble," Cal said.

I do want a story though.

After another period of silence and pacing, Ted finally spoke.

"I've chosen you to be the scribe. My scribe. The one who records the truth about what is really happening with Charles Robinson, PacLabs and performance enhancing drugs."

"So that's what all this is about?"

"That's just the collateral damage. I'll get to ground zero in a minute."

Cal didn't like the sound of that. *Ground zero? Is there another figurative bomb that Ted is about to drop?*

"Tell me what I need to know to write this story."

This time, Ted didn't measure his words.

"What you need to know is that Charles Robinson is a ruthless man who will do anything to protect his evil empire!"

Cal remained calm despite Ted's voice rising 10 decibel points with each new response.

"What's so evil about it?"

"I think you know the answer to all this, but I'll give it to you straight and unfiltered."

Cal flipped the page and waited for Ted to begin.

"Before I begin wading into all the gory details, I want to know if you found my thumb drive at the bowling alley?"

"I did."

"And did you get a chance to look at it?"

"Sure did. It generated quite a few questions I wanted to ask you about today."

"Good. We'll get to all that in a moment. For now, let's go back to the beginning, the moment when my life began spinning on its axis."

CHAPTER 35

KELLY GAVE UP TRYING to reach Cal. Despite her repeated efforts to get him on the phone, her calls kept going to voicemail.

"What is wrong with him? Why won't he answer my calls?"

She pulled into Cal's apartment complex and parked in one of his two allotted spaces. Cal's guilty pleasure purchase when he moved to San Francisco was a convertible Fiat 500. He said he needed a car that helped him drink in San Francisco when he was putting around town. It wasn't long before he realized all he was drinking in were fumes as most of the times traffic slowed to a crawl. He decided to use it only for weekend getaways to Yosemite or a sea coast drive along the 101. That all meant Kelly had a car whenever she needed one while visiting Cal.

She activated the mechanism that closed the top before turning the engine off.

Bounding up the stairs to Cal's second floor apartment overlooking the San Francisco Bay, she stopped for a moment to bask in the sunlight. It was breezier than usual, but at least there wasn't any smog strangling her lungs like a typical day in L.A. She needed to relax, even if for just a moment. The stress of the past week had worn her down.

She stared at a barge creeping through the bay before she snapped out of her daze.

It all makes sense now!

Then she gasped in horror.

This meeting with Ted IS a trap!

She opened the door to Cal's apartment and began furiously dialing his number. Nothing but voicemail.

Then she remembered she could find where Cal was if his phone was still on. It was a long shot, but she thought she'd give it a try anyway. Nothing else was working.

She opened Cal's laptop and began rooting around in his applications folder for the Find iPhone app. Cal's creativity achieved new heights when it came to leaving his phone in random places. He once left it inside a pot while cleaning up the kitchen. Another time he put it in the freezer on top of an ice cream carton before finding it with ice crystals forming on the screen two hours later. Kelly often lost her phone too but didn't have to stress about it anymore after Cal showed her how to use the app. If the phone was on, it would locate where your phone was, providing as detailed of a location as possible using the GPS mechanism in the phone.

"Come on! Come on!" she yelled at the laptop as the compass spinning on the screen told her it was searching for Cal's phone.

After a few seconds, a map popped up with his location. He was at a warehouse on the corner of Third Street and Marin.

She began dialing the San Francisco Police Department.

CHAPTER 36

CAL SHIFTED IN HIS SEAT, situating himself for a long note-taking session. Despite Ted waving a gun recklessly in his direction, he felt surprisingly at ease. This was Cal's element. A man wanted to tell a story and he would listen. Cal would've listened with or without the gun. As Ted began to talk, Cal almost forgot about it. *Almost.*

"None of this was an accident," Ted said.

"None of what?" Cal asked.

"Everything. Everything you see. Everything I've done. It's not a coincidence."

"Then tell me what *it* is?"

"*It* is the matermind of Charles Robinson. Every last detail of my life over the past few years was something he dreamed up, something he controlled."

"So you work for Charles Robinson?" Cal asked.

"Who doesn't work for him? All of L.A. and half of California works for the man in some way or another. You even worked for him."

"But you work for him more closely?"

"You could call it that. He recruited me for this job."

Cal flipped the page in his notebook, mostly out of habit. He hadn't even filled a page or written anything of consequence, but he grew restless of Ted's shrouded babblings.

"You said you wanted to start at the beginning, so let's go there."

"Fine," Ted said. "The beginning is the day I killed my parents. Up until that day, I was a pretty normal 14-year-old boy. At least, I thought I was normal. I thought every kid got beat by his dad when he was drunk. Every single night. Then I found out that wasn't so normal. I mean a few other kids got beat by their dad too. But nobody had the problems I had with my mom."

"What did she do?"

"She molested me. She started with me when I was at such a young age that I never really questioned it. But as I got older, I found out, that certainly wasn't normal."

"So what happened?"

"One night after my dad beat me real good, I pulled out some chloroform I stole from my high school's chemistry lab. I waited until they were already asleep and then smothered them with it to make sure they were knocked out. Then I doused them both with gasoline and burned the house to the ground. I heard them screaming when they woke up in time to realize it was too late. I always told people they died in a crash. It was easier that way for me, making up some story instead of saying that they died in a fire and dredging up my past."

"And the cops didn't charge you with murder?"

"No. I got a sympathetic detective. I even told him what I did and why I did it. He filled out his report that it was an accident."

"So nobody ever found out?"

"He must have told somebody because Charles Robinson knew when he first approached me."

"Approached you about what?"

"About working for him, of course. He wanted to buy our little company, DigiTest. We had an unbeatable test that would catch PED users. We were sitting on a gold mine. We started looking for prospective buyers. That's when I first met Robinson."

"He wanted to buy your company?"

"Yeah, but not for the reasons you might think. He wanted to control things, including who got caught and who didn't. He didn't want to use our program – he wanted to bury it."

"So he bought you out?"

"Yeah, but he approached me first, black mailing me within fifteen minutes of meeting me. He said he would help me save my brother if I'd do him a favor and make sure all the partners agreed to the sale. He knew my brother was dying and that I'd do anything to save him. So, I agreed and coereced the other partners to sell to Robinson. However, that wasn't all. He then asked me to help kill my other partners, make it look like accidents. And if I didn't, he said he'd tell them I was a murderer. He told me that if I'd done it before, I could do it again – especially if Tommy's life depended on it."

"So you did it?"

"I had no choice. I made them all look like accidents, except for Trevor Wyatt. He was always gambling so that it was easy to do a straight hit on him. The official story was that he was in debt, but the reality was I was under the control of Charles Robinson and my brother's life depended on it. So I did what I had to do."

Cal stopped writing just long enough to flip another page in his notebook.

"And the job at PacLabs?"

"Oh, I do work there. But the real work I do is for Robinson. Whenever he calls, I have to do his bidding."

"What kind of bidding?"

"I think you know."

"I think so too, but for the record?"

"For the record, I mostly beat people up. Coercion might be a more respectable name. But I just convince people they need to do what Robinson wants them to do."

"But it's more than that sometimes, right?"

"On a few occassions, I've been known to step over the line."

"That's what those big payments were for? Hit jobs?"

"You could call them that. Robinson likes to call it the last resort. He'd much rather work with willing pawns, though sometimes it's necessary to 'trim the loose ends,' as he likes to call it.'"

"So what were all those failed drug test forms that you gave me? What was that about?"

Ted paused, looked down, and then pushed the barrel of his revolver down on the desk in front of him. He then looked up at Cal.

"I'm getting to that."

CHAPTER 37

THE WOMAN IN DISPATCH who answered Kelly's call took her time in assessing the situation. A freaked out reporter who thinks her friend is in danger and is walking into the trap set by a hitman for the most powerful businessman in California? Kelly knew she sounded like a fool as she was saying it. But judging from the dispatcher's ambivalent response, Kelly imagined that the dispatcher pictured her with a tinfoil hat. Just another crazy calling the San Francisco Police Department.

Kelly jumped into the Fiat and typed the address into her phone. She needed directions now. If the police weren't going to be there for Cal, she would.

Her phone estimated it would take twelve minutes to get there.

Kelly tapped nervously on the steering wheel when she came to a red light.

Come on! Come on! I don't have time for this!

Just like a few other adventures with Cal, this one started innocently enough. A whistleblower leaks information. Cal begins digging. Boom!

These investigations usually went off without much more than a whimper. People loved to deny everything until you presented them with facts. That was what usually made people talk. When they knew their dirty laundry was going to be aired, they might as well do it their way as opposed to letting some journalist misconstrue the facts. It often softened the brunt of the truth. But not this time. Everyone denied everything, preferring to sweep the truth into the graves of the truth tellers.

Kelly pulled into the parking lot and noticed Cal's car was the only one there. She put the car in park and waited for a few moments. She didn't have a plan as to what she would do once she walked in the building—or if she even could do anything at all.

As she mulled over a plan, she never saw the black towncar park along the side of the road. Nor did she realize it had been following her the entire way there.

CHAPTER 38

CAL REALIZED HALF THE PAD in his hand was already covered in notes. If Ted took much longer to get to the crux of the story, he might not be able to capture it on paper.

Ted ran his free hand through his hair, refusing to set the gun down for even a moment. By this time, Cal had grown accustomed to the constant threat of the gun being waved about that he hardly noticed it any more. Except when it was pointed at him.

Cal flipped another page and looked up to see the barrel of Ted's revolver aimed right at him.

"I know you don't really care about me," Ted said, shaking the gun at Cal. "What you really want to know about are those drug tests – or should I say, failed drug tests? That's more accurate anyway."

Cal began to relax just a bit.

"So, is that what you did at PacLabs? Conduct PED tests from samples?"

"Yeah. Not real glamorous, I know. But that was my paycheck—my very small paycheck in comparison."

"So what was going on?"

"Robinson had rigged the system."

"In what way?"

"He suppressed the tests that failed each week. That is, he suppressed them if they paid."

"Who paid?"

"The other owners. We sent a list to him each week. After a day or two, he would instruct us to bury all of the failed drug tests and replace them with fake passing results."

"So, if a team paid to keep it quiet, nobody knew about it?"

"Exactly. The few players who were busted over the past few years happened only when a team told Robinson to let the player get busted. If you review the short list of players suspended for using banned substances, almost every one of them was a troublemaker in the locker room—or someone who wasn't performing. I even had a couple of requests to falsify a failed drug test to get rid of players that teams didn't want around any longer."

"So, why bring that information to me?"

"Because I wanted out. I thought I could escape this mess. Then the more I thought about it, the more I realized that it was never going to end. I was always going to be haunted by this. Eventually you would write a story and I would be connected to PacLabs. My name would've been smeared, even if I would've figured out a way to avoid legal charges."

"Maybe. Most of the time, the guys on the bottom rung make plea deals and escape serious time. I know a guy who could help you with that."

Ted began pacing furiously, back and forth, taking two or three steps in each direction before reverting back the other way. He tapped his forehead with the gun, thinking as he ranted out loud.

"Don't you get it, Cal? This is never going to go away for me. Especially not after you write this story."

"I don't have to write *everything*," Cal answered, hoping to loosen Ted's lips even more.

"It doesn't matter!" Ted screamed. "I'm as good as dead—and you might be too!"

The stress of Ted's confession—as well as the guilt—

weighed more heavily on Ted as he revealed more and more. And Cal grew more nervous with each passing moment. He wasn't ready to die. Not today or any time soon. Especially with Charles Robinson walking around as a free man.

"Well, if I'm going to die, Ted, you at least ought to tell me what happened to Aaron Banks? Did you kill him?"

"No, that was Bobby Franklin's doing."

Slackjawed, Cal stared at Ted. "Bobby Franklin? Aaron's agent? He's the one who killed Aaron?"

"Not him personally, but he took care of it. He knew where Aaron met his PED supplier. Hired a hit man. Simple as that."

"But why kill him?"

"Charles Robinson threatened him, even told him they were releasing Aaron," Ted said. "They were through with him and wanted a more productive player at a lower cost. The Stars barely fit all their superstars under the salaray cap anyway so they were looking for a way to reduce some extra baggage. Robinson offered Franklin the equivalent of his cut as if Aaron had signed a big five-year deal. Apparently, Franklin took him up on it, warning him that if he didn't go along with it, Robinson would leak Aaron's failed drug tests—along with the failed drug tests of half the players on Franklin's client roster."

"And how do you know all this?"

"Franklin tried to hire me, but Robinson told me not to since it could be linked back to him at some point. But I wouldn't have done it anyway. I loved watching Aaron Banks play. He was one of my favorite players when he was in his prime."

Cal had more than enough for a national front page news story. This transcended sports. A murder-for-hire plot that included an owner, an agent and one of his players. But there was still something that nagged Cal, leaving a few questions that he needed answers to fit into a bigger theory he proposed.

"But why make it look like a suicide? Less of a mess? Why

not stage it as a robbery or something more random that might happen to a guy cruising around in a McLaren F1 in L.A.?"

"I'm not sure why, but Robinson always had his reasons. Nothing he did was random. It's always calculated and precise with him. He's just—"

Ted stopped talking. He quit pacing, too. He looked down at the ground as if he was searching for the word – or the courage to say something.

"Like when he told me to lure you here today so I could kill you," Ted said, glaring at Cal.

Cal looked up from his paper and didn't have a chance to move.

Bam!

CHAPTER 39

KELLY HEARD THE SHOT ring out from the warehouse. *Why aren't the cops here?* Running into the building went against her better instincts—but she did it anyway. There was no way she would sit a hundred feet away while he bled to death from a gun shot wound. She prepared herself for the worst.

Her thoughts raced faster than her feet and she raced toward the door.

What if he's dead? What if Ted shoots me, too? What if they try to frame me for his murder?

She couldn't dismiss the thoughts fast enough before another horrible scenario presented itself.

By the time she reached the door and yanked on the handle, she was already panting. She wasn't sure if it was due to hyperventilation or overexertion. The amount of time it took her to reach the door would've given Usain Bolt a surprising challenge.

Kelly flung the door open and could see only one thing— the body sprawled out on the floor with blood pooling around the head. Her mouth agape, Kelly covered it with her right hand, muffling her scream. The scene horrified her. Blood spatters to the right of the body. Flesh peeled back near a bloody gaping wound.

It was the body of Ted Simpson.

Once it finally registered with Kelly that the body wasn't Cal, she scanned the room for him.

"Oh, Kelly!" Cal said.

He rushed across the room in her direction before suddenly stopping.

Confused, Kelly tried to read the expression on Cal's face. It was one of horror. It was one she didn't quite understand until a firm hand clothed in a black leather glove wrapped around her mouth and another arm whipped around her stomach, clutching her tight.

"Talk about making this easy," the man's voice snarled.

Kelly struggled but to no avail. The man's presence was enough to command Cal's respect, if not outright fear.

She didn't recognize his voice. But Cal did.

"Charles," Cal said.

CHAPTER 40

IN A GAME OF POKER, it's challenging to get the other players to fold if they don't believe you have all the cards. If they think you're bluffing, they'll go all in and call your bluff. Cal was playing the consummate poker player, the wild gambler named Charles Robinson who always felt he had the best hand at the table, even when he didn't. And he always won. But Cal was ready to go all in—he just didn't expect the stakes to be so high.

What is she doing here?

Cal tried to calm down and deal rationally with the fact that the woman he loved was standing in front of him with a gun to her head. He needed to keep his hand close at this point. Even Robinson wouldn't believe him if he showed him all his cards.

"Let her go! She's got nothing to do with this," Cal finally stammered.

Robinson just glared at Cal, choosing to remain silent.

Frustrated, Cal repeated his demand. "I said let her go. She's meaningless to you."

This time, Robinson responded.

"Of course, she's meaningless to me, but you aren't. And since she means everything to you, I figured this is the best way to get you to do what I want."

"And what do you want?"

"I want you to disappear. You, Kelly, all your notes, all your dreams of winning a Pulitzer. Poof! I want them all gone. You're messing with my plan, my legacy. And I don't like it when things get in the way. Fortunately, Ted made things a little bit easier with his cowardly stunt here. Now, you're all that's left between me and billions of dollars."

"What more could you possibly want? Don't you already have everything a man could want?"

"Perhaps, I do. But I don't have everything I can have. And if I can have more, I'm going to have it. And come Monday, I'm going to have billions more."

Cal seized on Robinson's bravado and his California-sized ego. "What's happening Monday?"

"Cal, Cal, Cal. And you call yourself a journalist? Don't play coy with me. I know you know what's happening Monday—unless you're completely inept."

Cal knew exactly what was happening Monday and how it would result in another huge windfall for Robinson. But he wanted to make Robinson say it. He needed his hunch confirmed—like any good Pulitzer-winning reporter would do.

"Humor me," Cal said.

Robinson said nothing. Still clutching Kelly, he instead moved toward Ted's dead body and grabbed the revolver from his hand. He emptied the chamber as the bullets clinked on the cement floor. Then he moved with Kelly toward Cal.

"Here. Take it," Robinson said, offering the gun to Cal.

Cal didn't move, refusing to offer his hand.

"If you don't play along, Cal, there are many other ways this could end. Perhaps it'll be a murder-suicide after a contentious breakup when the police find a break up email sent from Ms. Mendoza's account to yours. I can make that all happen. Or there are other ways to involve other people you love."

Still reluctant, Cal forced his left hand forward, hoping Robinson wouldn't realize it.

"Do you take me for an idiot? I know you're right handed. Other hand!"

Cal felt he had no choice. He also watched his winning hand transforming into a losing one—and all the chips were sitting in the middle of the table in the form of Kelly.

How is this happening?

Cal felt the cold metal in his hands. It was an object that demanded respect. It was an object that gave one power. It was an object that served as protection. But for Cal, it was an object that weighed on him, perhaps even an Albatross that he could never explain away in a million years to a responding officer who just so happened to be on Robinson's payroll. He knew the charges wouldn't stick, but even to be accused in a case of this magnitude would cause him enough problems.

Once Cal took the revolver, Robinson continued.

"Now that I know nobody will believe a disgraced reporter who just so happens to be a murderer, I'll be happy to tell you how Monday will be a big pay day for me."

Kelly suddenly began squirming. Her quick movements annoyed Robinson, compelling him to press the barrel of his gun into her temple. She stopped as suddenly as she began.

"Does this have anything to do with Head Gear?" Cal asked.

Robinson smiled.

"I see you aren't so inept after all," Robinson said.

Cal kept pushing.

"The public offering of Head Gear on Monday? That's what this is all about?"

With each revelation of Robinson's self-imposed brilliance, Cal watched the owner swell with more pride. It was brazen behavior, if anything.

"Sssshhh," Robinson said, holding his index finger up to his mouth. "We don't want to let out this little secret."

"Which one? The one about your son-in-law shielding you by investing your money in Head Gear? Or the one about you blackmailing a man with his brother's life to turn him into an assassin? Or maybe the one about your hiding PED usage of certain football players?"

Robinson looked down at Ted's dead body and shook his head.

"And you, Mr. Cal Murphy, are the reason why I own media companies. A dilligent little cub reporter like yourself just might poke his nose where it doesn't belong. And we wouldn't want you spreading such scintilating accusations in a respectable newspaper, now would we?"

Kelly, who had been compliant for most of their tête-à-tête, squirmed in an attempt to break free.

Cal said nothing as Robinson pressed his gun forcefully into her temple.

"Now, now, little lady. We'll get to you in a minute," Robinson said.

Time started to run short for Cal. He needed to throw his hand on the table. He needed to force Robinson to show his, even though the gun appeared to be the winning wildcard. If he could keep the focus on himself, maybe Kelly would be safe.

"I will promise not to write anything if you let us walk away," Cal said.

Robinson snickered.

"I think we're way past that point. You had a chance to walk away when your boss told you to stop pushing this story. But you didn't listen. You only have yourself to blame now—for both your death and the death of this pretty little lady right here."

Cal decided it was the right moment to give his conciliatory speech—one that was anything but that in reality.

"You're right. I guess I should've walked away from a story about a blackmailing billionaire controlling NFL drug testing and assassinating potential roadblocks to his plan to cash in on a fear he stoked regarding head injuries."

Robinson smiled.

"You forgot to the add the part about how I got away with it."

CHAPTER 41

CAL GRIMMACED AT ROBINSON'S COMMENT. *Is there something I could have possibly forgotten? Could Robinson have snuffed out any of his plan? This plan was airtight. This isn't happening.*

Despite Robinson's newfound bravado, Cal decided to stay the course. He was going all in.

Time to put all the cards on the table.

"*You* forgot the part where all of this was broadcast live over the Internet," Cal quipped.

The comment didn't seem to phase Robinson. He paused and grinned.

"You think I didn't see you talking to Marty Price in the press box on Sunday?" Robinson shot back. "I approached him after you left and told him if he called you to let me know and I'd make it worth his while not to publish anything you gave him."

Cal nervously rocked from one foot to the other. He still hadn't thrown his last card.

"I hope you called Miles Kennedy, too."

His final salvo launched, Cal waited for·any number of outcomes, only one of which he wanted to see: total surrender.

Robinson remained stoic, forcing a smile that left Cal wondering if he was outsmarted by the consummate opportunist. His phone began beeping incessantly. One, two, three. Alerts one right after the other lit up his phone. He resisted the urge to answer.

194 | R.J. PATTERSON

"I think those are your friends telling you to put a sock in it," Cal said, smirking triumphantly.

"Well played, Cal. Too bad it's not going to save your life or hers."

With his retort, Robinson shoved Kelly away, shooting her in the back. He then took aim at Cal, firing off three rounds before sprinting toward the door.

Outside the building was an FBI SWAT team awaiting Robinson. The hostage situation broadcast live over the Internet was enough for Kennedy to convince the FBI that his former reporter needed assistance.

Robinson immediately threw his hands in the air and dropped his gun as FBI agents descended upon him. Smothered into the parking lot gravel, Robinson surrendered without a struggle. For all his bluster, Robinson wasn't willing to go down in a firestorm of bullets. A media mogul done in by new media.

As the agents cuffed Robinson's hands behind his backs, a blood curdling scream ripped through the parking lot.

"Noooooooo! No! No! No!"

It was Cal's voice.

CHAPTER 42

INSTEAD OF RAKING in the chips that was Robinson's arrogant bravado, Cal was left on the dirty floor begging for Kelly's life. He could barely see her limp body through the tears flowing out of his eyes. No story was worth this pain and anguish. No writing award could make up for the loss of the woman he loved.

Cal fell to his knees next to Kelly, begging her to hold on. There wasn't much else he could do except pray. And he wasn't very good at that, though he regretted his sporadic contact with the Almighty in the moment.

"God, no!" Cal cried.

Two FBI agents rushed in and began performing CPR on Kelly in an effort to revive her. The seconds ticked by like hours for Cal as he wailed.

It wasn't supposed to happen like this. Kelly wasn't supposed to be here. Why was she here anyway?

A million questions flooded Cal's mind. He couldn't begin to dismiss them fast enough before another one presented itself.

Cal grabbed Kelly's hand and pleaded with her.

"Hang on, baby! I know you can do it!"

Just then, Cal felt a slight squeeze from Kelly. Her eyes opened and she looked at him.

At this point, nothing was for certain, but Cal took it as a good sign.

"Don't worry. We'll take care of her," said one of the attending FBI agents.

Moments later, a medical response team swarmed into the room, stretcher in tow. Cal felt Kelly squeeze his hand once more before the paramedics whisked her away and into a vehicle headed for a nearby hospital. Cal wanted to go but was restrained by an FBI agent.

"We need you here, Cal," he said. "We've got some important questions for you. She'll be alright."

Cal hoped the agent was right.

CHAPTER 43

FBI AGENTS PULLED CAL aside and began routine questioning. Cal asked for a moment alone before delving into such matters. Nothing seemed important to him other than Kelly. However, he couldn't ignore his phone, which rattled with texts and voice messages. He dug into his pocket to retrieve his cell phone and get the perspective of those who had helped him orchestrate the dramatic live takedown of Charles Robinson.

He punched in Miles Kennedy's number without listening to his voice message.

"That was spectacular!" Kennedy said.

Cal knew how the drama must have played on a live web stream, but he didn't feel the same way—not yet, anyway. Kelly was lying in a hospital somewhere fighting for her life.

"So you captured it all?" Cal asked.

"Every last second. I can't believe it. If you don't win some sort of award for this, that will render all awards meaningless in my book. Simply incredible. And to think you weren't a fan of new media?"

Cal appreciated Kennedy's support and enthusiasm. But at the moment, none of it seemed to matter much to him.

"I'm still worried about Kelly," Cal replied.

"Is she gonna make it?"

"That's what the paramedic told me—but she lost a lot of blood. I've got to get to the hospital and be by her side."

"She'll make it, Cal. And don't worry—what you did today was an incredible act of heroism and journalism. If I ever get the chance, I'm going to hire you back."

Cal smiled. He didn't care about his job at that moment. All he cared about was Kelly. But it was nice to hear Kennedy say such kind words about him, especially since Cal's actions nearly cost Kennedy his job, too.

* * *

The ride to the hospital would have been faster in a horse and carriage. At least, that's what Cal thought as the black government-issued Chevy Tahoe caught every red light over the seven-mile drive to UCSF Medical Center. He reflected over his adventures with Kelly from the past. She somehow managed to worm her way into life-threatening situations with him, yet she always escaped unscathed. But not this time. The image of her limp body oozing blood onto the warehouse floor seared into his memory. He couldn't shake it no matter how hard he tried. And the anxious ride to the hospital only gave him more time to replay how he could have kept her out of harm's way.

When Cal arrived at the hospital, the medical staff directed him to the waiting room. Kelly entered surgery as soon as she arrived and the prognosis was grim. The sheer amount of blood lost put her survival in doubt. Cal slumped into a waiting room chair and stared at his feet. He glanced around the room only to notice it was full of others as glum as himself. As the minutes ticked by, all Cal could do was think about how amazing Kelly was.

Kelly was as independent as they come, a pure bred Idaho woman through and through. Her nose for a good story spelled her downfall this time. Cal had picked up on the link between Robinson and Head Gear. It wasn't until he listened to his voicemail from Kelly that he realized it was scandalous, too. An inferior product using endorsements bought with hush money.

Robinson was no fool. Public offering on Monday—stock sold within a month. He was already angling to avoid blame once Head Gear faced its first lawsuit.

That was Kelly's all-important contribution to the investigation, one that not only would assist in the ultimate takedown of Charles Robinson but also nuke Head Gear's initial public offering. While photojournalists don't exactly garner much respect by their newsroom brethren, Kelly had it. She earned it with instincts on par with a veteran reporter.

But she also possessed some other important qualities, some that pushed this case from a hunch to a full-blown conspiracy. She had people skills. Kelly, not Cal, convinced Mrs. Banks that exhuming her son's body was necessary to prove he was murdered and help clear his name. And she held Mrs. Banks' hand when watching her son's lifeless body get sliced open on the medical examiner's table was too much to bear. It was kind-hearted Kelly at her finest.

Another hand grabbed Cal's cold sweaty palm and squeezed it, snapping Cal from his stupor. He looked up. It was Mrs. Banks.

CHAPTER 44

"MAY I JOIN YOU?" Mrs. Banks asked.

Cal nodded, gesturing to the open seat next to him. He glanced at her and forced a slight smile before staring back down at his feet.

"She's gonna make it, you know," Mrs. Banks said, trying to start the conversation.

Cal remained motionless.

Mrs. Banks pressed on.

"You know why she's going to make it?"

Cal said nothing.

"She's going to make it because she has something to fight for. She has someone to fight for."

Cal resisted the urge to reply. *How can she be so sure? What does she know about Kelly?*

"You're probably wondering how I know that. I know you are. When you were examining Aaron's body after our talk and I just couldn't take it any more, she sat with me. I asked her what brought joy in her life. And you know what she said?"

Cal slowly raised his head and looked at Mrs. Banks in the eye for the first time. He still said nothing.

"She said *you*. She told me about how exciting it is to be with you and how satisfying it is to track down stories that rip the mask off evil and expose it to the world."

Cal looked back down at the ground again and wondered

to himself if she would say the same thing tomorrow. It's not very exciting to be used as a pawn by some evil power broker in a high-stakes game. Yet, that's what she was. And Robinson decided to fold like a coward, shooting a woman in the back. Cal pondered the reality of the situation and wanted to lash out at Mrs. Banks. But he couldn't. She was too kind, too compassionate. And she had just ventured through the worst living hell a mother could conceive.

"She loves you, Cal. She told me not only with her words but in the way she spoke about you. And you know what my pastor says about love?"

Cal shook his head, still staring at the ground. He wasn't sure he wanted to hear a sermon, but he didn't want to show Mrs. Banks any disrespect. So he invited her response.

"He said that we need to believe what the Bible says about love, true love. Not the mushy, gushy love—what real love is all about. He said, 'Love never gives up, never loses faith, is always hopeful, and endures through every circumstance.' You think this doesn't fall under the 'every circumstance' category here, Cal? Kelly loves you and she's going to endure, if for no other reason than her deep love for you."

Cal knew Mrs. Banks' words should have made him feel better, but he wasn't feeling it. Not when Kelly was banging on death's doorstep in a room just down the hall. Not when God seemed to abandon Kelly in her hour of need. At least, that's what Cal thought as he pondered how he might feel about an outcome that resulted in her death. It wouldn't be fair—and he didn't want to hear about God right now.

Mrs. Banks let her thoughts sink in before finally stunning Cal.

"If you love her, Cal, you won't give up."

Cal looked back up and stared at Mrs. Banks. Tears welled up in his eyes. He *had* given up. *Was it written on my face? How did she know?* Cal determined to believe. It was all he could do. That and pray.

Mrs. Banks got up and rubbed Cal's head.

"You hang in there, Mr. Cal Murphy," Mrs. Banks said. "You're a pretty special guy. And you gave me hope when I didn't have any. Don't you give up hope yourself."

With that salvo, Mrs. Banks got up and walked away. Cal watched as she walked down the hallway and disappeared. She helped him realize that true love doesn't lose hope, even in the darkest hour. She helped him realize that he truly loved Kelly.

Just then a doctor dressed in light blue operating room scrubs approached Cal.

"Are you Cal Murphy?" the doctor asked.

Cal nodded.

"Can I have a word with you in private? It's about Kelly."

CHAPTER 45

MILES KENNEDY STARED at the newsroom television. Channel 5, the local station owned by Robinson's media conglomerate, only had the guts to run a breaking news alert on the bottom of its regularly-scheduled programming, announcing Robinson's arrest in a deadly hostage situation with police. But not Channel 7.

Like circling sharks in bloody waters, Channel 7 unleashed on Robinson. It shouldn't have come as a surprise to anyone. The station was chocked full of reporters who had escaped the auspices of Robinson's heavy-handed approach to media coverage. Many of them joked that they worked at the California Pravda before working for a real news station. Kennedy knew many of the station's reporters, including Stacy Hartwick, who was dishing the emerging details live and on Twitter.

Kennedy grabbed an empty reporter's chair and sat down, putting his hands behind his head and propping his feet up on the desk. He wasn't smug about his role in taking down Robinson. Just proud that he participated in one of the most dramatic takedowns in new media history. He never imagined the picture provided by Cal's cell phone would provide such an incredible behind-the-scenes picture of Robinson's sinister side. Nor did he think it would take such a dramatic turn and show a person being taken hostage and shot.

Before Cal contacted him and shared his wild plan to stream

the entire event live, Kennedy wondered how much longer he could work for such a news organization. He even sent out a few resumes, some which might be getting a longer look at the moment considering his role in the story of the year. But Cal's idea was his own Hail Mary. Already finished in California if Robinson's vendetta was to be believed, Cal had nothing to lose. Kennedy, however, did. But he bought in to Cal's crazy plan and wanted to make history, something they did with quite a bit of flair.

As Kennedy sat enjoying the public defrocking of Robinson and his media's empire, he didn't see his editor storming down the hall toward him.

"Kennedy! In my office—now!" he roared.

Kennedy jerked up out of his seat and followed his boss, who stomped his way across the newsroom to his office.

The next 15 minutes qualified as verbal abuse. Kennedy's editor subjected his sports editor to every possible four-letter word and then some. Plenty of rhetorical, "How could you?" and "Who do you think you are?" questions. The door remained shut, but his editor's voice was so loud that it surely reached auditory levels throughout the newsroom. Kennedy kept waiting for his editor to take a breath so he could announce that he quit before the tirade ended with, "You're fired, Kennedy!"

Kennedy didn't care about his job. What he did care about were his people, especially his people who still upheld the tenets of respectable journalism. He cared about people who breathed journalism. He cared about people like Cal, who cared so much about the craft of journalism that he never stopped chasing the story even when he had nowhere to print it.

Reporters gawked and stared at Kennedy as he walked through the newsroom. He even smiled, wallowing in his new-found freedom.

Hardman shot a disapproving glance at Kennedy, who couldn't wait to unload on him.

"You think I did something wrong, Hardman," Kennedy said, stooping toward him and invading his personal space.

Hardman remained quiet as he drew back, using his feet to roll his chair deeper into his cubicle.

"You wouldn't know real journalism if it hit you in the face. And, yeah, I know you stole all of Cal's tips last week. You only wish you were half the journalist he is."

Kennedy then spun and continued down the aisle toward his office. He slammed the door and sat down, rooting around for an empty box to gather his things with.

He noticed he had five new emails in his inbox, four from other papers around the country. News wires burned up trying to disseminate this incredible story, one that Kennedy directed to be broadcast live on the paper's website.

Kennedy halted what he was doing to read the messages in his inbox. The first one was from his IT guy who said social media pushed more than eight million unique visitors to the website to watch Cal's confrontation with Ted and then Robinson.

Cal's initial plan was to get Ted Simpson to confess live. Whether he told the truth or not was a matter for the authorities to decide, but it would certainly create a hedge of protection around Cal. If anything happened to him in the coming weeks, Robinson would be a prime suspect. But neither Kennedy—nor Cal—ever expected Robinson to waltz through the door after a dramatic suicide by his assassin and then shoot a woman in the back before trying to kill Cal. All caught live and streamed to the web.

The rest of the IT guy's email said he had over 500 requests forwarded to him already, requesting footage of the streamed webcast.

Kennedy smiled and glanced at the next group of unread emails. Houston, Atlanta, Kansas City and Orlando—all great places to live and great newspapers to work for. All requesting an interview. He hated to leave San Francisco, but he knew it would be for the best.

He was eager to resume packing but couldn't stop thinking about Cal. He wanted to get to the hospital to see how he was doing. He would get there soon enough. Instead, he texted Cal telling him that he would be there soon. He also wondered if Cal might be interested in moving east a few thousand miles.

CHAPTER 46

THE COLOR DRAINED from Cal's face as he stepped into a private consultation room with the operating doctor. Cal didn't pray regularly or very often at all. But he was praying now, begging God that he didn't have to hear those dreaded words: "I'm sorry, Mr. Murphy. There was nothing we could do." Cal wanted to freeze the moment, the moment when he knew hope was alive. It seemed strange but at least it was better than pressing forward with a crushing reality—a reality without Kelly.

Cal decided he wanted to get it over with, one way or another.

"Out with it, doc. Is she gonna make it?" Cal asked.

"Kelly lost a lot of blood when she got shot—"

"Just tell me if she's gonna be OK or not!" Cal felt his desperation to know rise with every nuanced statement or evasive action. He wanted this news like he reported his own—straight and to the point.

"It's hard to say, but we think she's going to pull through," the doctor replied.

Cal exhaled, crumpling into a chair to his left. He knew there was more, but a giant heaping of hope gave him reason to believe the future—the future he imagined with Kelly—was still possible.

"We had to induce her into a coma to give her body more time to heal, but she's stable for now and we should know more tomorrow when we plan on waking her up."

Cal thanked the doctor and heeded his advice to go home and get some rest. More than anything Cal wanted to see Kelly's beautiful face again. He wanted to gaze at her while she slept, slide his hand along the brown tendrils surrounding her face. But it would have to wait. Apparently, there would be time for that later, time Cal wasn't sure existed twenty minutes ago.

* * *

Cal pulled into his apartment complex just after seven o'clock in the evening, craving something to eat and a good night's sleep. He planned to order out from the rib shack down the street and wash it down with a cold beer or two. Without Kelly around, he still wanted to celebrate Robinson's demise. But doing it alone didn't seem right. Maybe Kennedy could join him.

However, Cal never made it out of his car. For all his years of reporting on stories, he never actually considered the fact that he was putting himself into the same one he was covering. Journalists of every stripe—TV crews, radio reporters, magazine and newspaper scribes—descended upon his car with cameras and microphones, demanding to know more details.

"How do you feel?" and "How did you come up with this plan?" and "Did this have anything to do with your public spat last Sunday?" and a hundred other unintelligible questions flooded Cal's ears.

Why he never saw this sudden spotlight coming was a true testament to his journalistic focus and integrity. He was so focused on doing exactly what these reporters were doing—getting the story—that he didn't have time to consider the consequences of his actions. Not for him. And certainly not for Kelly.

Then he responded with the same words he loathed to hear while covering a big story: "No comment."

Cal didn't even roll his window down, mouthing the words

through the glass to the pack of reporters. With what felt like 5,000 watts of lighting glaring in his face, surely his comment was discernible.

He slowly reversed his car and raced out of his apartment complex. Dinner would have to be to-go on this night. And he wouldn't be eating it at his apartment either.

He needed a place to crash. He needed a friend who understood him. He needed Kelly. But Kennedy would have to suffice tonight.

CHAPTER 47

CAL AWOKE THE NEXT MORNING on Kennedy's couch to the slobbery wet kisses from Montana, Kennedy's frisky golden retriever. The sun glinted off the bay, alerting Cal to the fact that Friday morning rush hour had been in full stride for a while now—and he wasn't going to spend a second in it.

"What time is it?" Cal moaned. If it was before 10, he thought he would scream.

Kennedy chuckled as he scarfed down a bagel and cream cheese.

"10:30, sleepy head," Kennedy said.

Cal sighed, relieved that it wasn't too early, nor had he slept the day away. He still had some work to do, like delivering a final report with all the supporting evidence to respectable website that would take his story. He figured *The New York Times* was respectable enough and he had pitched his story the night before over email. He checked his email on his phone and smiled at the response agreeing to run his story. The fee for keeping this story an exclusive made Cal hoot out loud.

"Do you always wake up this happy?" Kennedy asked, turning a page in the newspaper in front of him.

"I haven't had much to be happy about lately, but this freelance gig from *The New York Times* is changing that."

Cal shoved his phone in front of Kennedy, pointing to the dollar figure on the screen.

"For one article?"

"It's *The New York Times*."

"I would've paid double that."

Cal grumbled something unintelligible.

"It's the sports story of the year if not the decade, for crying out loud. I would sell my kidney to have that as an exclusive," Kennedy said again.

Cal cared, but not too much to fight it. He needed to focus on pounding out a story worthy of the grand lady of journalism. It would be no small feat, but he had all the supporting evidence he needed. Bank records, drug testing documents, internal Head Gear emails, recorded confessions, black mail attempts. It was all there. Cal simply needed to sort it out and write one killer of a story.

The television in the background shifted to financial news. A reporter shared the stunning development surrounding Head Gear and how the initial public offering had been cancelled as federal officials opened an investigation into the company's business dealings. The reporter also went on to add that the NFL voided its recently-signed, multi-million dollar contract with the helmet provider. Cal smiled as he saw the wheels of common justice turning more swiftly than the court's.

"Would you mind running by my apartment and getting my mail for me since you don't have anything to do?" Cal asked.

"I get fired—thanks to you—and you think I'm suddenly your errand boy?" Kennedy asked.

Cal knew the outrage was feigned.

"Pretty please?" Cal asked, raising his voice several octaves to achieve the desired effect.

Kennedy finally agreed and mumbled something as Cal tossed him the key.

* * *

Kennedy returned in the early afternoon with Cal's mail.

"You haven't filed your story with *The Times* yet, have you?" Kennedy asked as he walked in the door.

"No. Why?"

Kennedy held up a piece of mail out of the stack of credit card offers and coupons he collected from Cal's mailbox.

"You got a letter from Ted Simpson."

Cal leaped from his chair and scrambled across the room toward Kennedy.

"Gimme that," he said, snatching the letter from Kennedy's hand.

Cal tore open the letter and began reading aloud.

> Dear Cal,
>
> First, let me begin by apologizing that you had to witness my gruesome death. I hope by now you've been able to figure out a way to use everything I told you and gave you to take down Charles Robinson. There's no way I was ever going to be free from that man. I felt like death was my only escape.
>
> However, that brings me to the point of my letter. While I was at peace with having to die, I don't feel that way about my brother. Robinson's goons will likely still try to have my brother removed from the special treatment facility. But I want him to still have a chance at life. He'll never have that if he's removed from the experimental treatment.
>
> From what I understand, he might be able to leave the facility in the coming months. To that end, I set up a trust fund in your name to care for my brother, Tommy. It truly is a trust fund since I am trusting you to use it on my brother's health care costs. I feel comfortable asking you to do this since you are the person I came to in the first place. I had

216 | R.J. PATTERSON

to trust you all along—and I'm doing it again.

Enclosed is a page detailing the name and contact information for my lawyer who helped set all this up. He'll give you instructions on where to direct funds for Tommy. I'm hoping there will even be some left in there when he gets released to help him start a new life.

Thanks for everything!

Warmest regards,

Ted

"Wow!" Cal said. "I thought I was thorough. This guy didn't miss a trick."

"It's exactly what I would expect from someone who collected enough goods on Charles Robinson to bring him down," Kennedy said.

Cal returned to writing and took intermittent breaks to eavesdrop on Kennedy's phone interviews with several newspapers. Kennedy was a pro and he would find a home somewhere. Cal hoped it would be soon—and he hoped Kennedy would be true to his word and hire him again. More than anything, Cal hoped it would be somewhere warm—and that Kelly could go with him.

CHAPTER 48

CAL REREAD HIS FINAL STORY one more time before attaching it to an email and sending it to his contact at *The New York Times*. He then took digital pictures with his camera of all the supporting documents. The story would run in Sunday's paper, giving the staff enough time to fact check everything and undoubtedly make sure everything was fine with the legal department. When he heard the sound of the final email swooshing into Internet fibers headed for New York City, Cal sat back in his chair. His satisfaction felt muted by the absence of Kelly.

Cal grabbed his coat and decided to go to the hospital alone. Kennedy volunteered to accompany him but Cal had some thinking to do. Plus Cal didn't want anyone else around but him when she woke up.

* * *

At the hospital, Cal met with one of the doctors who told him they had just woken her up for the first time thirty minutes ago. She was responding well and talking. The doctor cautioned Cal to go easy on her, trying to avoid stressful conversation. Cal agreed and proceeded toward Kelly's room.

He paused before opening the door, struggling to enter. Staring at her weak body in a tangled mess of tubes and wires, Cal stopped. He knew he did this to her. Technically, it was Charles Robinson. But in reality, Cal had dragged her into one of his foolhardy investigations and she was the one who got hurt, not him. He vowed not to do this to her again. At least not as his girlfriend.

Finally, Cal softly entered the room.

He commenced with the generic small talk as he settled down next to her bed. Cal held her hand, ignoring the tubes criss-crossing into her arm. She squeezed his hand, tilting her head and just staring at him and smiling.

"I'm so sorry, Kelly," he finally stammered.

"Sorry for what?"

"Sorry that I put you in this situation. Sorry that you're lying in a hospital bed and I'm not. Sorry that—"

"Sssshhhh," Kelly said as she cut him off and jammed her index finger to his lips. "Guilt be gone. I'm alive and I'm with you now. Let's just enjoy this moment, however awkward I may appear right now."

The corners of Cal's mouth turned upward slightly into a grin. This was the Kelly he loved, a woman who was intent on revelling in a moment of just being together. It was a moment he didn't want to end either. Ever.

"OK, Kelly. But before I just sit here and enjoy being next to you, I have a couple of questions for you."

"Cal, the intestigative reporter. His work is never done," Kelly said, chiding him.

"I'm serious, Kelly."

"Serious about what?"

"Serious about my two questions."

"OK, shoot."

Cal took Kelly's hand and looked at it. He wanted to gently caress it but decided maneuvering around such a jumbled mess of tubes and wires would only make the moment awkward.

Then he mustered up his nerve and continued.

"So, my first question is how would you feel about moving east?"

Kelly shot him a look of disbelief, mouth agape.

Before she could utter another word, Cal continued.

"My second question is how would you feel about marrying me?"

THE END

Thank you for adding *Better Off Dead* to your library. If you liked *Better Off Dead*, I would appreciate it if you would leave a review at Amazon, even if it's only a few words. It will make a big difference for me and other readers considering whether to buy this book. Thanks again!

NEWSLETTER SIGNUP

If you would like to stay up to date on R.J. Patterson's latest writing projects with his periodic newsletter, sign up at:

www.RJPbooks.com.

ACKNOWLEDGMENTS

So many people have been such an encouragement to me in this journey of writing novels. If it weren't for the valuable input of so many people mentioned below, this project would have never seen the light of day.

I must always start out by thanking my parents, who instilled in me the love for good stories and the art of good storytelling.

I also want to thank Aaron Patterson and Chris White, who have been great sounding boards in talking about story ideas and plots.

I appreciate the editorial assistance of Brooke Turbyfill and her keen eye in making this book better than it was.

And last but not least, I appreciate my wife, Janel, for giving me the time to help make this book a reality.

ABOUT THE AUTHOR

R.J. PATTERSON is an award-winning writer living in southeastern Idaho. He first began his illustrious writing career as a sports journalist, recording his exploits on the soccer fields in England as a young boy. Then when his father told him that people would pay him to watch sports if he would write about what he saw, he went all in. He landed his first writing job at age 15 as a sports writer for a daily newspaper in Orangeburg, S.C. He later attended earned a degree in newspaper journalism from the University of Georgia, where he took a job covering high school sports for the award-winning *Athens Banner-Herald* and *Daily News*.

He later became the sports editor of *The Valdosta Daily Times* before working in the magazine world as an editor and freelance journalist. He has won numerous writing awards, including a national award for his investigative reporting on a sordid tale surrounding an NCAA investigation over the University of Georgia football program.

R.J. enjoys the great outdoors of the Northwest while living there with his wife and three children. He still follows sports closely.

He also loves connecting with readers and would love to hear from you. To stay updated about future projects, connect with him over Facebook, on Twitter (@MrRJPatterson) or on the interwebs at:

www.RJPbooks.com

94716497R00136

Made in the USA
Columbia, SC
29 April 2018